SHERLOCK HOLMES
AND THE PLAGUE OF
DRACULA

SHERLOCK HOLMES AND THE PLAGUE OF DRACULA

by
Stephen Seitz

Mountainside Press

ISBN: 978-0-9708693-5-7

Book design and layout by Shakespeare, Inc.

10 9 8 7 6 5 4 3 2

Library of Congress Cataloging-in-Publication Data
Library of Congress Control Number: 2006934241

Mountainside Press
P.O. Box 407
Shaftsbury, VT 05262
Phone: (802) 447-7094
FAX: (802) 447-2611
E-mail: mntnside@comcast.net
www.mountainsidepress.com

TABLE OF CONTENTS

Acknowledgments

I would like to thank the following for their help and support: Bob and Sally Sugarman in particular for taking this project on; Jeanne Cavelos, whose sharp eye for error and authorial missteps turned this novel from a hobby into an actual story; and my wife, Susan Austin, for unflagging love and support.

S.S.

INTRODUCTION

For years, devotees of Sherlock Holmes and Dr. John H. Watson have been searching for Watson's fabled tin dispatch box, last known to be in the care of Cox & Company in London. That box contained Watson's notes and records of his cases of Sherlock Holmes. Indeed, many stories have been written claiming to have been based on the documents contained therein. But there is one problem with those stories: the Charing Cross branch of Cox & Company was obliterated by Nazi bombs during World War II. Watson's records went with it.

However, that does not mean everything was lost. Watson was a compulsive scribbler, and kept a daily journal, which he first mentions in *A Study in Scarlet*. The doings of his life naturally included his adventures with Sherlock Holmes, and that journal survives.

How do I know this? Because those volumes sit next to me as this very moment as I write this. I have no doubt of their authenticity; they have passed a series of extremely expensive chemical tests and handwriting analyses. There are plenty of extant samples of Watson's handwriting; once he became famous, many of his patients kept his prescriptions so they could have his autograph. I am also convinced that Watson is the physician most responsible for the bad reputation doctors have for poor handwriting. If only he'd used a typewriter!

I come by these volumes (almost) honestly; Watson

left his estate and belongings to Sherlock Holmes after his death in London in 1929, at the age of 77. Holmes put them into storage and forgot about them.

They come to me because my great-aunt married a man named Holmes, who turned out to be a distant relative. Both Sherlock Holmes and his brother Mycroft died childless. Neither death has ever been announced, and my every inquiry has hit a very British brick wall. I doubt we'll ever know when or how Mycroft died. But Sherlock lived into his ninetieth year, leaving this world in 1944, serving his country to the end.

His estate had to be settled, and luckily my great-uncle was stationed in England when he received word that, so far as could be determined, he was Sherlock Holmes' closest relation. He did not care; a farmer from the hills of upstate New York, he had no idea who Sherlock Holmes was, but was grateful to have the farm at Sussex Downs, its contents, and of course, the money. My great-uncle sold the farm. Luckily, he was also an incurable pack rat. He took everything else back home in case he could use anything on his own farm; the Holmes hives, in fact, are still producing honey. What Uncle Bob couldn't use went into the attic.

On a family visit when I was ten, I was playing up there when I came across a musty old trunk, one of several. I tugged at the lock, but it didn't give. That aroused my curiosity, and the more the lock refused to budge, the more determined I was to break it. Finally, I found an old toolbox, grabbed a screwdriver, and snapped the brittle tin.

Inside, a treasure trove: a heavy revolver, many scribbled pages of manuscript, a dried snakeskin, fake beards and moustaches, but mostly copybooks. The scrapbooks, notes for monographs, the never-completed *Whole Art of*

Detection, The Practical Handbook of Bee Culture, so much more.

In the other trunks, I found manuscripts, letters, memoranda, newspaper clippings, all kinds of tobacco apparatus, an ancient hypodermic—everything but Holmes' famous Stradivarius. (My great-aunt persuaded Bob to donate it to the Smithsonian. The violin on display there may well have once belonged to Sherlock Holmes.)

I opened one of the copybooks and discovered I could barely read it. The handwriting was atrocious, and I wasn't accustomed to Watson's usage then, so I took it home and stuck it on a shelf. Several years passed, and I discovered *The Hound of the Baskervilles,* which quotes Watson's journal extensively. That rang a bell, and I examined the long-forgotten volume. The journal extracts quoted in *Hound* came right from the journal in my lap; they were not much changed in the final publication.

I have since hauled all the combined personal effects and extant papers of Holmes and Watson to my home in Vermont. In Watson's daily journal is the first draft of Holmes' cases, as they occurred day by day, as well as details of the unchronicled cases Watson hinted at from time to time. Once Watson realized how intense interest in Holmes had become, he kept separate, more detailed notes of his experiences for publication, while using the journal to keep track of events in his own life.

I have also learned the extent to which Watson changed things to suit his stories. Names, dates, and places; often, Watson transplanted events from one case into the published account of another. It was necessary to do so; with every word, Watson was at great risk of libel.

For example, Watson knew of Professor James

Moriarty and his right-hand man Colonel Sebastian Moran well before "The Final Problem." Moriarty and Moran both appear in *The Valley of Fear*, which took place in 1887, but was published in 1914. However, "The Final Problem," which appeared in 1893, was Watson's first published account of Moriarty. Watson pretended he had never heard of Moriarty in order to tell a better story.

What you now have in your hands is extraordinary: how Holmes and Watson became enmeshed in the notorious case of Count Dracula. In general, I have retained the epistolary form used in *Dracula*, quoting directly from the sources, rewriting and paraphrasing mostly for the sake of clarity. Happily, there has been no difficulty in securing outside documentation for the Dracula story; the Harker, Godalming and Seward papers have been freely available for years, and I have used them where they fit into the story. Most of the Harker and Seward entries appear here for the first time. To obtain them, I contacted the British law firm my family used to settle the Holmes estate in England—the one founded by Peter Hawkins, in fact, known today as Hawkins, Harker, Graham & McFarlane. Their tireless researchers were able to find the letters, journals, and newspaper clippings I needed, and more. (Amanda Keswick's note to her parents, for instance, was stuck to the back of an RSVP pasted in her wedding album.) All other entries are from Watson's journal or letters unless otherwise noted. I have peppered the text with footnotes where appropriate; I hope the reader will not find these overly intrusive.

I should note that I have left out a lot. Watson wrote everything down, including the details of his generally mundane daily life when he was away from Baker Street.

In his journal he comes across as a stronger personality than he did in the Sherlock Holmes memoirs; as often as not, Holmes turned to Watson for a medical opinion, but in the Canon Holmes seems to know all and even instructs Watson. Again, Watson sacrificed accuracy for a better story. Watson's own modesty has forever enhanced the reputation of Sherlock Holmes, and I hope we can help correct the record a little. Watson was far more than a sounding board in the partnership.

There are twenty of the journals, covering the years 1886 to 1927, and fascinating reading they often make. Besides filling in the gaps of the Sherlock Holmes saga, we find many of the missing details of Watson's own life: his second career as a police surgeon, the story of his stormy third marriage later in life, his experiences in Afghanistan and in World War I, the death of his brother, and more. If there is sufficient interest, perhaps additional sections of the journal might see publication.

—Stephen Seitz
Springfield, Vt.

PART ONE

CASTLE DRACULA

CHAPTER ONE: MINA MURRAY

Letter, Dr. John H. Watson to Mary Watson

August 3, 1890

Dear Mary,

Holmes is dozing, so I am taking this opportunity to explain my actions over the last few days. I apologise for the suddenness of our leave-taking and for the hasty note I left. But you must admit that our domestic life of late has been somewhat strained, and your increasing visits to Mrs. Forrester I can only view as escape from my company. The situation is wearying me, so when Sherlock Holmes asked me to accompany him to Transylvania, I must say it was with considerable relief that I accepted.

You are still my wife, however, and I hope this time apart will give our hearts a chance to heal, and to cleave together once again on my return. It is only fair that I give you an account of my doings while I am away. I will post this missive when the train stops at Trieste.

As you know, last Wednesday I called on Holmes at Baker Street after visiting a patient who lives nearby. Naturally, he called me in before I had a chance to knock.

"My dear Watson, how good of you to come!" he said. "Your visit could not be more fortuitous. I am expecting a client. Tea?"

A steaming pot and two cups had already been set out, and Holmes fetched a third. I could see this anticipated client was about to break a spell of tedium for my friend.

When Holmes is bored, he tends to slouch around the flat in his mouse-coloured dressing-gown, hunting through newspapers for sensational items of interest, looking like nothing so much as a heron with its wings clipped.

Holmes had been indoors too long; his normally pale complexion seemed even whiter than the last time I had seen him, and his long, thin fingers were stained yellow, a sure sign that he had been smoking more cigarettes than usual. His grey eyes were sharp and bright with anticipation, and he paced about the room with determination.

Today he was smartly dressed in tweeds and tie. The thick stack of unanswered correspondence usually affixed to the top of the mantel with a rusty jackknife was gone. He had shelved his books and indexed his documents. Some sort of malodorous chemical experiment was also in progress on the acid-stained laboratory table by the window, which, mercifully, was open. (The aromas emanating from your kitchen are far preferable to those from Holmes' often rammish chemical investigations.) I confess that hearing the familiar bustling sounds of Baker Street's traffic from the window stung me with nostalgia, for I've hardly seen Holmes since the wedding. I took my accustomed armchair by the fireplace, with a burst of anticipation as I did so. For while a stable, domestic life has its charms, one does sometimes miss the hunt.

Holmes offered me a cigar from the coal scuttle.

"Her name is Mina Murray," Holmes said. "She believes her fiancée, Jonathan Harker, is in deep trouble somewhere in Transylvania, and she suspects he may have come to harm. We are to find him."

"We?"

"If you care to come. You're bored, my dear Watson.

You suspect the patient you just left—your first visit this morning, if I'm not mistaken—is a hypochondriac, and I flatter myself that you took this patient as an excuse to visit. Besides, you've lost five pounds since our visits to Wisteria Lodge, and your face lit up like a schoolboy's when I said I was expecting a client."

"He's not a hypochondriac, exactly, but he does tend to inflate the importance of his ailments. How did you know? And why the first?"

"You usually start your rounds at eight. It's a little after nine now, hardly time for more than one examination. Your bag is still locked, which tells me you have not yet opened it. There are no finger marks on your top hat, where I see your stethoscope is in its accustomed place. Having touched neither, I perceive that you either diagnosed the patient's problem at once and solved it on the spot, or that you diagnosed no problem whatever."

"His complexion told all. He's allergic to paprika, but did not know it. It has been a dull summer, Holmes."

"Perhaps we can relieve our *ennui*, for Miss Murray is now approaching."

The door opened, and the page introduced a slender, dark-eyed woman of medium height, sharp, bird-like features, and fine chestnut hair tucked into a chignon. Her practical air and modest, unassuming dress marked her as a governess or secretary. I wondered if her fiancée had simply run off with a fiery gipsy woman. I know what a taste of the exotic can do to a man. (Think where would we be, Mary, without the Agra treasure and the Sign of Four. I'm grateful that you enjoyed my account of the case more than Holmes did.)

"Oh, you're a doctor," she said on learning my name. "Do you know anything about somnambulism?"

"Precious little," I admitted. "My wife has been given to bouts of it lately. It is usually a symptom of something else. Do you often walk in your sleep?"

"I never have," she said. "I am staying with a close friend who has been suffering from it."

"I can examine her if you—"

"Pray sit down," Holmes said, offering her the sofa while he took the armchair opposite. "What may I do for you?"

"As I explained to you in my letter," she said, "I have reason to believe that something terrible may have happened to my poor Jonathan, who, as I may have mentioned, is a junior solicitor, working in the employ of Peter Hawkins—"

"Ah, you did not tell me that," Holmes said. "Has Mr. Harker ever mentioned a Professor James Moriarty to you?"

My ears pricked at once.

"Yes," Miss Murray replied. "He is one of Mr. Hawkins' clients, and apparently an important one, for Mr. Hawkins handles all his matters personally. But beyond that, I know nothing about him."

Holmes nodded and lit a cigarette. "Pray continue, Miss Murray. Please give me every detail, and be as precise as you can."

"Though Jonathan is the most junior member of the firm, Mr. Hawkins selected him for a most important assignment," she said, as if she had prepared a speech. "A certain Count Dracula, of Transylvania, is purchasing an estate by the name of Carfax, in Purfleet. Mr. Hawkins' firm was engaged to find a suitable property for the Count and make the arrangements. This was done, and all that remained was getting the Count's signature on the contracts."

"Do we know why this Count Dracula did not come to England himself?" asked Holmes.

Miss Murray shook her head. "He was willing to pay Jonathan's expenses and he provided a handsome retainer," she said. "Jonathan left for Munich at the end of April."

"Why do you think he has come to harm? Has he not written?"

"At every train stop, but after he arrived in Transylvania his letters became sporadic."

"That could be explained by an inefficient postal system. The trains are notorious in that part of Europe. I take it you have brought some of his letters?"

"Yes." She opened her handbag and extracted two. "One is to Mr. Hawkins, and one is to me. I would expect the letter to Mr. Hawkins to be brief and businesslike, which it is, but so is the one he wrote me, and that is not like him. And neither letter is in his usual style."

"Did you bring any of his other letters?"

She handed over what she had. Holmes examined the first few and shrugged. But the letter dated June 12 arrested his attention.

"Here, Watson, take a look at this."

It read:

My dearest Mina,

How delightful is the spring in Transylvania! Every bush, every tree, all of Nature is alive with promise. Lest I forget springtime in England, however, the time has come at last for me to return to my land and my beloved. Please forgive me for staying away so long.

My business with Count Dracula is concluded and I shall soon be in Bistritz and on my way home.

With all my love,
Jonathan

The letter to Hawkins was dated June 19, and read simply:

All is finished with Count Dracula. He has signed all the contracts, I have answered all his questions, and prepared for the business he plans to conduct once he reaches England. I am advised that he will be sailing from Varna sometime in the next few weeks. It is to be hoped that I will have the pleasure of acting as the Count's representative once I am safe on native soil. I am sorry to be so brief, but my carriage awaits.

Jonathan Harker

"As you can see, Mr. Holmes, these aren't like the others. They're too short, for one thing. Jonathan writes pages, especially if we have been separated for any length of time. That paean to spring makes no sense whatsoever. Normally, Jonathan would have told me he was on his way home, and then described his recent adventures. He would not have used 'with all my love' as a closing salutation; we say, 'your loving.' This one sounds so ... final."

Holmes nodded. "Please let me have his itinerary," he said.

Miss Murray gave him a neat, typewritten document listing Harker's route, hotel reservations, and train schedule.

"What does Mr. Hawkins have to say about this situation?"

"He is as concerned for Jonathan's safety as I am; sometimes I think even more so. He feels a tremendous sense of responsibility for Jonathan. The Harker and Hawkins families have been friendly for years, and it was only natural for Jonathan to join the firm. Mr. Hawkins suggested I contact you, and he has offered to pay your expenses and fee."

"Thank you, Miss Murray, I will consider it. Do you mind leaving the letters and the itinerary?"

"Of course not," she said.

"We will look for him, Miss Murray. Unfortunately, I have other pressing business at present, but I do not think a few extra days will make a difference at this point. I shall contact you when I have made plans."

Though somewhat disappointed, she said, "Thank you, Mr. Holmes."

"One other thing. Pray do not discuss your visit here with anyone just yet, even Mr. Hawkins. A little silence may prove helpful in our investigations."

She assented.

"You are a good and noble woman, Miss Murray," said Holmes as he showed her to the door. "I envy your students."

"My students?" she ejaculated. "Who told you I had students?"

Holmes replied, "You have a firm command of factual data, and a clear and confident manner of speech. You say precisely what you mean, which facilitates clear understanding. You are also accustomed to choosing, and even making, your own clothes, which indicates both frugality and a small income. You do not defer to men; I infer from this that you have had to keep a number of little boys in line, given your youth. 'Schoolmistress' is the inevitable conclusion. I also note that you are a touch typist and frequently act as your future husband's secretary."

"Remarkable," she said, her dark eyes widening a little. "In fact, I am an assistant schoolmistress, and I do act as Jonathan's secretary when needed. If anyone can find out what happened to Jonathan, surely you are he."

"We'll be in touch shortly," he said, closing the door. Turning to me, he said, "Can your patients spare you for a bit, Watson?"

"Of course." I scribbled a note and gave it to Billy, explaining to my next patient that I would be late.

"A question of my own, Miss Murray," I said. "Are you any relation to Sergeant Josiah Murray, who served at the Battle of Maiwand?"

"Not that I know of, Dr. Watson," she replied, and left.

"Professor Moriarty's lawyer," I said after her tread faded from the stairway. "What could he want with a Transylvanian nobleman?"

"There may be no connection whatsoever," Holmes replied, lighting a cigarette, "except for Hawkins' willingness to pay my expenses. The fact that he works for Moriarty raises my suspicions. They could have come to me before this. Why send me to Transylvania to look for

Jonathan Harker at this particular moment? I can only believe that the good professor wants me out of his hair for a while."

"If he had any."

"Harker is likely acting for Moriarty, whether he knows it or not. What do you make of Miss Murray's story, Watson?"

"Wait. How did you know she was a touch typist?"

"Someone who only uses one or two fingers often has blunted fingertips. Hers were all smooth, yet the itinerary is neat and free of error."

"Ah. Well, I see no reason not to believe her story, but I also see no reason to assume any harm has befallen young Harker."

"Young Harker?"

"I am assuming he and Miss Murray are of close ages. He is a junior solicitor, and this is his first assignment. Anyone can collect a few signatures. It is not a job that requires wisdom and experience."

"Well done, Watson."

Holmes emptied the packet Mina Murray had left behind. Besides the letters and itinerary, there was a photograph of Jonathan Harker. I judged him to be about five-and-twenty. His hair was dark and brushed back, and he had pale eyes and a rather weak chin. Women would not be naturally drawn to him, but he clearly sparked something in Mina.

"Well, she's right about the letters," Holmes said, handing me one about ten pages thick. "It's quite chatty, and flush with the usual endearments." He made that latter observation with the slight distaste he always holds for the tender emotions.

"Which illustrates what I have been saying all along," I said. "He may be trying to let her down gently. The region is rife with gipsies, and gipsy women are intense and passionate. Perhaps one of them took a fancy to Jonathan. That, and a warm spring day in an exotic land, and you have romance. But it is difficult to break off an engagement, and, in this letter, he could not bring himself to do it directly. Still, he has to tell Mina sometime. The closing salutation may indeed have been a goodbye, and once Harker claims his gipsy bride, he will send a long, sorrowful letter to Mina, breaking her heart."

Holmes burst into laughter and applauded. "Bravo, Watson! You've done it again! No wonder your readers love you!"

"I take it I am wrong in every particular."

Holmes chuckled, stuffing tobacco into his pipe. "You offer a perfectly valid interpretation that has nothing whatsoever to do with the facts. Take another look at the letter, in light of what Mina Murray told us of Harker's writing style. I take it you found the first paragraph to speak of newfound love?"

"Well, yes."

"Please read it again."

"'How delightful is the spring in Transylvania!'" I read aloud. "'Every bush, every tree, all of Nature is alive with promise. Lest I forget springtime in England, however, the time has come at last for me to return to my land and my beloved. Please forgive me for staying away so long.'"

"Does that sound remotely natural to you?" Holmes asked. "If it were any more stilted, it would be a circus act."

I persisted in my theory. "Mina may still be beloved,

but that doesn't mean he plans to marry her anymore. A man may love two women, Holmes. He's lying to her."

"Actually, his message is quite clear if you read the first letters of each sentence."

I did: H-E-L-P.

I sighed in frustration. "Why do I bother, Holmes?"

"Because these exercises sharpen your mind, Watson. You simply apply your observational powers differently. You're a doctor, not a detective. Thus, your skills as a diagnostician have grown considerably during our association; surely the instant discovery of your most recent patient's allergy demonstrates that. I have heard your praises sung many times. Certainly I would not trust my own medical care to anyone else."

This soothed me somewhat, though I always marvel at that nimble mind of his.

"What you should do now, Watson, is finish your rounds for today and make preparations for someone to take your practice for the next month. We leave for Transylvania in the morning."

"I thought you had pressing business."

"I am throwing off a scent; she'll report to Hawkins, of course. I'm sure Moriarty's up to something, but it shouldn't take too long to determine what it is and turn it over to the city police. There is no doubt in my mind that this Dracula is holding Harker prisoner, and may be doing so at the behest of Professor Moriarty. And if this is so, Harker will likely be in need of medical attention, if he is still alive. I'll have Gregson keep a close eye on the professor while we're out of town."

And so, my dear, you now know as much as I do. Holmes has been remarkably uncommunicative, and we have mostly passed our time chatting, reading and playing cards. He eyes my journal with suspicion, and I am weary wondering what it is he is keeping from me.

The train is pulling into the station for a layover, and Holmes is beginning to stir. I must conclude. May this letter find you well, and know my thoughts and prayers are ever with you.

Your loving,
John

CHAPTER TWO: BISTRITZ

Dr. Watson's Journal

August 8, 1890

Alone at last. Misleading my readers is one thing; misleading my wife is something else.

The true reason I was in Baker Street was not a coincident patient living nearby, though that was certainly true, but so that I could ask Holmes to give me an answer to a tormenting question: does Mary have a lover?

I have run the facts over and over in my mind, lay awake until the early hours, agonized with not knowing. We have not had marital relations in weeks; indeed, I have not seen Mary even a little unclothed since the last time. There is distance between us where there once was passion.

"My good fellow!" Holmes said on opening the door, perceiving my difficulties at once. "What has happened? Has Mrs. Watson left you?"

"I fear she is about to, Holmes. How did you know?"

"Because no one is taking care of you, my dear chap. Your hat has not been brushed, there is a small bloodstain on your tie from a shaving nick you forgot to plaster, you haven't slept a full night in at least two weeks, and you've lost five pounds. When both a professional man and his wife neglect his appearance in such a manner, I can only conclude marital discord."

I am pleased to say that my friend gave my story his full concentration.

"Why do you believe she has taken a lover?" Holmes asked, cigarette aglow.

"It goes back to the fact that, try though we might, she has been unable to conceive a child," I replied. "That's what first put a strain on our marriage. Since then she has grown distant and colder. She rejects my advances. She finds excuses not to be near me."

"But you've seen no illicit correspondence? Detected another man's cologne on her clothing, anything like that? Have you followed her?"

"No, but— Holmes, I couldn't bear to see my wife in another man's arms!"

Holmes laid his pale, slender hand on my arm.

"Of course you can't. I'll ease your mind, Watson, one way or another. You'll have an answer in the morning. Then it's off to Roumania."

But Holmes didn't have an answer in the morning. Mary stayed at home all day, and now I wait in agony. I almost pray for a telegram telling me she's ending the marriage.

Holmes and I are now in the Golden Krone Hotel in Bistritz, an ancient border town that is the last stop before the Borgo Pass and the road to Castle Dracula. The country is rugged and beautiful; I have had much time to study it, for the trains are so slow they may as well be pulled by oxen.

The mountains are lovely, green with summer, though some are capped with bright, white snow. Often, they are topped by old castles that cry out this region's long history of war with the Turks and with various tribes from the east. The modern world has intruded so little here that its manifestations sometimes seem bizarre. The peasants wear the thick mustaches, baggy trousers, white linens and wide leather belts I would expect, but a number of them also wear wide-brimmed hats that look as though they were imported directly from the American Wild West.

Bistritz itself is the gateway to the Borgo Pass and is surrounded by gray, ruined stone battlements. Settled by the descendants of Attila the Hun and constantly threatened by the Turks, the region's harsh experience with foreign invaders is visible everywhere. Indeed, to judge by the architecture, time stopped sometime in the reign of Henry VII.

For Holmes, it has been a busy trip. He has been interviewing conductors, porters, stationmasters, and passengers. (Which reminds me; Holmes did solve a pretty little problem for one of our fellow passengers with two conversations and some astonishing deductions. I must include it if I ever publish another of our adventures.) We have firmly established one thing: Jonathan Harker has not returned along the route from whence he came. I had mentioned this possibility to Holmes when we left Switzerland two days ago.

Since then, the case has taken a decidedly sinister turn. Either Mina Murray does not know her betrothed very well, or we are after the wrong man. The Harker who has been described to us is nothing less than a child-stealing monster.

Bad enough the train was four hours late, but we were told to expect that by nearly everyone we encountered along the way. I had thought normal suspicion of foreigners was behind our cool reception at the train station and at the hotel. Our businesslike tweeds marked us as metropolitan Englishmen right away, and we had trouble engaging a ride from the train station. Again, our fellow passengers told us this was normal.

Only when we arrived at the hotel did we learn the truth. The innkeepers are an elderly couple who call themselves Gustavus and Catherine. In his white shirtsleeves and suspenders and great white mustache, Gustavus looks every inch the *hostelier* he is; under her billowing aprons, Catherine wore a tight-fitting garment that would have flattered her had she been a woman far younger. With her high, proud cheekbones, flashing dark eyes with a touch of gipsy fire and flowing once-black hair, she must have been handsome in her youth.

We are fortunate that Holmes speaks German, and he has been kind enough to translate for me, but I had no difficulty understanding the initial conversation.

"You are Englishmen," Gustavus said.

"We are," replied Holmes, "and we'd like to stay the night. Two rooms, please."

Gustavus nodded to Catherine, who bustled away. "We had another Englishman here some months ago."

Holmes nodded and produced the photograph. Catherine gasped and crossed herself.

"You are too late," she said. "He is *nosferatu.*"

"He doesn't bathe?" Holmes asked.

The old woman shook her head. "Not unclean. Undead. He was here to visit Count Dracula, and has now become one with him."

"I don't know what you mean."

Gustavus brought us inside the ancient hostel and gave us harsh dark wine in earthen goblets. His face was stark with fear, and it was clear he did not know what to do.

"You must understand," Holmes said in German, "we are here in the service of the young woman who is to be Mr. Harker's wife. Her heart will be broken if we do not find him. Have you seen him since he stayed here?"

Gustavus shook his head. "He is dead, and not dead. He is *vampyr*."

It was all I could do to keep my tongue. To think, this close to the twentieth century, that such barbarous superstitions still hold sway in the world! Holmes and I exchanged a look, and a silence descended over the conversation. Once again, I had the feeling that we had somehow traveled back to the Middle Ages, when evil superstition gripped the hearts of all who lived here, where science was looked upon with suspicion as a dark art. Though history is replete with murderous madmen who believed themselves to be vampires (and Holmes has several volumes on this phenomenon in his peculiar library), they no more walk the earth than men do the moon.

Poor Gustavus looked at us with scepticism, as another pair of foreign imbeciles who would have to learn our lesson the hard way.

"What makes you think Mr. Harker has become a vampire?"

"Because he has been seen, *mein Herr*. He went to the Count's castle, and we heard of him no more for weeks. Then he appeared one night and stole a baby. Soon the baby's mother disappeared."

"You said you had not seen him yourself," replied Holmes. "How do you know it was Mr. Harker?"

"The baby's mother recognized his clothing. He was dressed just like yourselves."

"When did this happen?"

"The first attack happened toward the end of June," Gustavus said. "Many of my customers saw him after I closed the pub for the night. He was seen crawling out of the Kreski home."

"Did any of them know Harker?"

Gustavus shook his head.

"But his clothing gave him away?"

"As I told you."

"Where is the Kreski home?"

"You must not go there," said Catherine. "They have suffered terribly as it is. Please don't make them suffer more."

"Madam, if a murderer is loose, he must be brought to justice. I will see to that, vampire or not."

Catherine grabbed my arm, squeezing it with great force. "You must go no further!" she cried. "You don't believe! The Count has not walked among you! Herr Harker did not believe, and no one will carry his name now! Stop, and let that monster have no more power!"

I patted the woman's arm in my most doctorly manner, tried to look reassuring, and begged Holmes with my eyes to say something. Turning his attention to her, he said, "I'm sorry you lost your sons, and I know that what you had to do to bring them peace must have broken your heart. They would have grown into extraordinary men, I'm sure. But you must understand that we promised Mr. Harker's family that we would find him."

Catherine pulled back, fear in her eyes.

"Devil!" she spat. "How could you know these things?"

"Holmes!" I snapped. "Keep your deductions to yourself! Can't you see how this woman has suffered?"

With a nod, Holmes indicated the portraits of two young men, in age not more than twenty, in ornate frames near the kitchen door. They were the image of Gustavus.

"The portraits are placed where you alone are most

likely to look at them," he said. "You need them nearby, yet you do not share them with the public. There are no portraits of wives or grandchildren, no sign of any family here but yourselves. I conclude, therefore, that they have passed away. It is pure deduction, madam, not devilry."

"Don't you *Englisch* say the devil cites Scripture for his purpose?" she snarled, her hand curling about the rosary at her neck. Then, with a sudden gesture, she snapped a crucifix under Holmes' nose, startling him. He took it into his pale white palm and kissed it.

"As I promised, no devilry."

She paled, snorted and went into the kitchen.

Holmes, betraying his relief with a nervous smile, displayed his palm to Gustavus. "It is not burned," he said.

"You are a Christian gentleman?"

"Anglican."

"Not of the true Church," said Gustavus. "I remind you that your church was created by an earthly king, not the apostle of Christ."

Holmes poured another goblet for himself and Gustavus. I had hardly touched mine.

"Your sons died in the same year," he said. "What did Count Dracula have to do with it?"

It was now Gustavus' turn to turn pale. "You have powers of your own," he said.

Holmes did not deny it. "Please tell me," he said.

"Albert and Vlad," Gustavus said. "They were twins. Vlad would have been a priest. The love of Christ was strong in him. Albert was popular here, the customers liked him, and any girl in Bistritz would have been pleased to be his bride."

"But Dracula intervened."

"Have a care when you speak that name!" Gustavus ejaculated. "You use it too freely. We thought by naming one of our sons after him we might be spared. But Vlad chose to prove his devotion to the Lord Jesus by going to the castle to reclaim the Count's soul."

I could see tears forming in the man's tired red-veined eyes, and he struggled to continue.

"I apologise for this display, Herr Holmes," he said, draining his goblet and pouring more. "Vlad went to the castle and it was the last time we saw him alive. I knew what had happened, but I also knew the consequences of going to the castle. Albert called me a coward and went after him, even though he could persuade no one to join him."

"Did he disappear as well?"

"No. Three days later, I found him, near death, on the road to the Borgo Pass. Almost no part of his body was unbloodied. Deep bites and claw marks on his thighs, his arms, his ribs and belly. His nose was broken, and he could not stand. But his neck and breast were not touched. I know the Count allowed him to live."

"For what purpose?"

"As a warning to uninvited visitors like yourselves. But it was too late to save him."

"How did he die?"

"His wounds were too deep," the old man said with tears pooling in his eyes. "The flesh began to rot, and he wouldn't stop bleeding. Herr Holmes, it is a terrible thing to see your children die."

He cried again, and we let him weep. "We could not take a chance," Gustavus said at last, "but they should not have demanded that I do it!"

"Do what?"

"I— Albert was dead beyond doubt, but after three days, he would have become *vampyr* if nothing was done. I could not wish that for my son. The priest insisted that I be the one to …"

"To?"

Almost in a whisper, Gustavus said, "I … separated his head from his body. I stuffed the mouth with garlic, and I removed his heart for separate burial. Herr Holmes, his teeth were sharp as knife blades!"

"I am sorry for your ordeal," Holmes said gently. "What happened to Vlad?"

"A girl in the village reported seeing him. She would leave her family's home at night to meet him. He had clearly fallen from Christ. She started to waste away. She covered Vlad's bite marks on her breast and neck and became afraid of daylight, all the usual signs. But this time we were ready.

"We followed her to their meeting place in the forest. Poor Vlad was now in rags, any trace of the priest he would have been gone. He was now a wanton animal, attacking her breast with lust and hunger. We subdued them both with crucifixes and holy water, and … we decided it was best to end this plague on the spot. How foolish that hope proved to be."

"You killed them both?" Holmes was incredulous.

"Vlad was already dead, and the girl dying. This pestilence had to be stopped, Herr Holmes. We held them down, and … must I continue, Herr Holmes?"

"You will not rest easy in your mind unless you do," he said.

"We drove wooden stakes through their hearts. We cut

their heads off and stuffed them with garlic. Then we burned the bodies— right there in the woods."

We sat by our drinks in silence for a while, and Holmes said then, "I cannot tell you how sorry I am."

"You cannot defeat the Count. He controls the night and its creatures. Sooner or later he will have his way. Herr Harker is dead. If you find him, you must destroy him in the manner I described. It is the only way his soul will ever find peace."

We finished our drinks and went to bed; no one could eat after that, but a strong aroma of garlic emanated from the kitchen as we left.

I count it as a blessing that Harker has not been seen in the village in some time. I should hate to report to Miss Mina that her lover has been beheaded to pacify the natives. But I have every reason to believe now that is exactly what will happen if we don't find Harker first.

Holmes is now out in the village, and I am too agitated to sleep. Thoughts of my wife and her mystery lover torment me. Ordinarily, this adventure would be thrilling me, not killing me. Were I not afraid some careless remark of Holmes' might get him attacked, or worse, I would abandon him here and get back to whatever marriage I have left.

CHAPTER THREE: THE TRAIL OF JONATHAN HARKER

Dr. Watson's Journal

August 10, 1890

If the villagers are to be believed, Sherlock Holmes and I face our doom tonight, for as I write this we are the uninvited guests of Count Dracula. Holmes is poking about in the castle.

I don't see anything to fear. The castle, at least on first inspection, is completely deserted. There are no signs of activity. Dust covers the furniture, chickens roam freely in the courtyard, the gardens are overrun with weeds.

There are signs of recent habitation, however; we found a full larder, a functional kitchen and a cellar thankfully free of Roumanian wine.

But I will elaborate on the castle in due course. We are here a day later than we planned. The villagers flatly refused to take us, nor would they rent us either horses or the leiter-wagons that are the common means of transportation here. Though he won't admit it, Holmes' habit of deducing the details of a man's life from a few casual observations put the fear of Satan into them and cost us any allies we might have found. Many have been crossing themselves on our approach, and making gestures Catherine told us are meant to ward off the evil eye. Holmes, deaf to my personal agony, has been taking all this in good humour.

"What would they make of modern medicine?" he said. "Cure someone, Watson, and they'll burn you at the stake."

"Not before they drive one through your heart," I replied sourly.

No fewer than ten people offered us crucifixes, which we accepted to prove that we are not the spawn of Hell. Idolatrous though it may be, I find the one around my neck to be somewhat comforting. But if they trust in the crucifix so much, why do they still fear the Count?

Fortune smiled on us as the evening set, for it was then we found gipsies setting up camp on the outskirts of town.

"You seek the Count?" asked their bemused leader, a swarthy man with an imposing black mustache. He spoke English with a thick Hungarian accent, and gave his name as Janos.

"It may be necessary to speak to him," Holmes replied.

This cause much mirth among the gipsies.

"Then you should have stayed home," Janos said as the laughter subsided. "He left for London weeks ago. I myself prepared his shipments."

"Shipments?"

"Yes, yes. Gigantic boxes filled with common dirt. Where it took four of us to load one onto the wagons, the Count tossed them up like sacks of potatoes. He is a powerful man, Count Dracula."

"How many?"

"Forty, fifty, I don't really remember."

"Are you sure there was nothing else in the boxes?"

"We dropped three, and all that spilled out was earth and rocks. The Count said he planned to use them for agriculture on his new English estate."

"Did you see anyone else at the castle?"

Janos hesitated for a moment, and that's when we knew he'd spotted Harker.

"Staff? Servants?" prompted Holmes.

"We saw no one who should not have been there," he replied blandly.

Holmes suddenly displayed Harker's photograph, at which the gipsy blanched.

"We know he was there," Holmes said. "Was he alive?"

"Very much so," Janos said, slightly relieved. "The Count said he was an honoured guest, and not to be put to work. He threw letters to us."

"Oh? Where are these letters now?"

"We gave them to the Count. We were not going back to the village for days, while the Count makes frequent visits. He knows where they can be posted."

"You handed them over without reading them?"

"Of course."

"And you haven't been back to the castle since?"

Janos shook his head.

"We must go," said Holmes. "Can you take us and bring us back?"

"Have you gold?"

The haggling began, but when it comes to money, not even the greatest deductive mind is a match for a gipsy with an empty purse. We eventually settled on an outrageous price, and agreed to travel at the dawn.

"It is best," he said. "You will only need one night?"

"No more than two."

"Then we will stay with you."

"You're not afraid?"

Janos shook his head. "He is not at the castle."

And so we made our way through the forbidding

Borgo Pass and into the green, beautiful, and imposing mountains called the Carpathians.

The rather bumpy roads took us first past green farm plains, orchards, and peasants toiling in the fields, and I found it difficult to reconcile the warm golden sunshine and the sweet aromas of ripening plums and pears with the climate of fear in the village we left behind.

These eventually gave way to magnificent forests of oak, beech and pine as we ascended into the mountains themselves. Though not so immense as the mighty crags of the Kush Mountains which tower miles above Kabul, the Carpathians are solid and forbidding, the trees like rows of soldiers keeping eternal watch on this territory.

We barely spoke. Holmes sat in silence, glancing occasionally at the countryside, his brow furrowed, his mind lost in ratiocination. Even the gipsies, normally a chattersome lot, stilled their tongues as we clip-clopped through the forest shadows. The horses seemed reluctant, but they never faltered as we made our way slowly along the bumpy dirt road.

As the mountains grew ever higher on either side of us and began to intrude on the sun, I felt as though thick stone walls were closing in. The balmy temperatures of August diminished as we made our way, and by early afternoon it might as well have been November. I longed for my overcoat.

"See that one?" Janos said, as we passed a particularly notable tall mountain peak, glistening with recent snow at its summit. "If you're Christian men, you should cross yourselves now."

"Why?" I asked.

"That is God's Seat. From here, they tell me, He can

survey the world and decide where He is most needed. You may need His help soon, yes?"

I started to make the sign of the cross, but a glare from Holmes stopped me.

"We are not superstitious," he declared. "There are no villagers to mollify here. If the Almighty wants to see us, then He ought to know where we can be found."

Without realizing it, I fondled the crucifix around my neck.

"When in Roumania, Holmes ..."

He laughed, but as we progressed, we noted the occasional peasants we passed crossing themselves as we went by.

When we stopped so the gipsies could conduct some trade with farmers they knew, I joined them, needing to stretch my legs after the long climb in the carriage and to dig our overcoats from the luggage.

I spotted a cairn a bit off the road, at the base of a gargantuan boulder, and stepped over to examine it. As I did so, a young peasant woman, dressed in black linen and thick black aprons, with a black scarf holding her tresses close to her head approached me. But for her grief, she would have been lovely.

She uttered something in her native tongue, to which I could not respond. I stepped away from the stones, and she fell on her knees before them, weeping. One of the gipsy boys in our expedition touched my arm.

"She wants to know why you come here," he said, his English thick with accent.

"We're looking for someone," I replied.

The young woman rose, faced me, and asked another question, including the word "*Englisch*."

"'Are you English?'" the lad translated.

I nodded.

Another question: "'You seek the vampire English?'"

"We seek another Englishman," I replied. "I don't believe he is a vampire."

"He has been here," the boy translated, as the young woman brushed away a tear. "I lost my little Maria six weeks ago; we have lost so many children since he came. If you come to destroy him, then you are good men, men of honour. But you must be careful. The Count has gone, and he would not simply abandon his castle. The English vampire is keeping it for him."

I displayed my crucifix. She nodded.

"Have you seen him?" I asked.

The boy repeated my question and she shook her head.

"Maria was the last. Perhaps the monster is preying on the other side of the mountain, in Bukovina."

She began to cry. I comforted the poor woman as best I could, left her with the boy and joined my companion in the carriage.

"Another peasant who thinks Harker has stolen her child," I told Holmes, who was settling back into his seat. "This one was taken six weeks ago."

"That fits," Holmes said. "As you know, I have been asking about these child snatchings, and everyone agrees they stopped toward the end of June."

"You have a theory?"

"Not a very comforting one, but we have very little in the way of fact. I believe the Count disguised himself as Harker, and kidnapped and murdered these unfortunate children. So, if Harker somehow escaped, he would be dismembered by these peasants in the belief they were making their homes safe from vampires."

As we continued to ascend, I began to notice that as we saw fewer and fewer people, we saw more and more animals. Ravens seemed to mark our progress; twice I saw wolves sitting on their haunches, staring at us through the trees and following us with their bright red eyes, as if they knew we were coming and had reason to monitor our progress.

Temperatures dropped rapidly now, and the wind began to scrape our faces. We donned our overcoats as the trees thinned and eventually ceded their territory to cold, jagged, uninviting boulders. Even then, we never left the sight of wolf or raven, and the sensation of being watched made its home in my soul.

"Watson, look!" cried Holmes as we rounded a curve. "There it is!"

Above us loomed the outline of a magnificent stone ruin, battlements that had repelled Turks and Huns, the seat of cruel Wallachian rulers who brooked no challenges and impaled their traitors, watching them scream and welter in agony as they breakfasted ... perhaps in the very courtyard we soon would enter.

At least one wall had collapsed, and weather-worn, square-cut boulders started to appear along the ungraded road. Only now did I notice the late afternoon shadows growing across the mountains and the valleys beneath. Perhaps a painter like John Constable could do it justice. Below us were vast, forbidding forests, fertile fields and orchards. The peasants toiling in the fields seemed as small, industrious, and uncaring as ants. Dark shadows, rich and purple, crept along the landscape, swallowing it as the afternoon waned. I felt a chill in my bones that was unrelieved even when we finally gained the castle courtyard.

The courtyard had the look and air of abandonment. The grounds had not been tended; crows, pigeons and rats ran unhindered across the tufts of wild grass and bush that dotted the grounds. The windows were as dark as anthracite, and not a sound could be heard but from the panting horses and the howling wind.

"Pitch camp!" barked Janos.

"I think we'll sleep indoors, if it's all the same to you," Holmes said.

Janos stared at him in wonder.

"The Count may be gone, but he won't leave his home unguarded," he said. "As long as he needs gipsy labour we are safe, but how will you protect yourselves?"

Holmes pulled a crucifix from his pocket.

"A trinket like that won't keep the Prince of Darkness at bay," Janos said.

"I also have this." Holmes produced his hair-trigger pistol; I displayed my trusty Webley.

"Use silver bullets," Janos huffed, and we approached the massive wooden door to the great hall, which would not budge, push though we might. There was no knocker, no bell, no way to signal anyone who might have opened it. The ancient lock resisted Holmes' best efforts to open it. We must have wasted half an hour. Our exertions caused the gipsies much amusement. At last one of them took pity on us and gestured broadly from the stable, where the horses were being cleaned and fed. Inside was an unlocked door to the main building.

With a laugh, Holmes led the way inside. The door led to a storage room, where we found plenty of animal feed and similar supplies. Another door in the storage room led to a narrow hallway, which we followed to empty and dusty servants' quarters, and then to the kitchen. To our surprise, the pantry contained great smoked hams, bread, dried fruits, cheese, and other victuals that seemed to me, in my now famished state, like ambrosia.

"Well, let the gipsies have their horsemeat ragout," said Holmes, placing one of the hams on the counter. "It may not be English, but at least it is food I recognize."

"Aren't we going to tell them?"

"Of course, but they'll refuse. The count employs them; they won't wish to offend." He left to fetch wine, finding Tokay of acceptable vintage.

As Holmes predicted, the gipsies declined Count Dracula's food. After we supped, we expanded our explorations to the rest of the wing. We decided to start with the great hall, which was growing darker by the minute. The remains of giant logs lay in the fireplace, and they made me realize how cold the room was. We spent the next hour putting a fire together and lighting candles.

When we were done, eerie shadows danced every-where in the vast, ancient granite room. On one wall was an enormous and intricate tapestry, depicting the history of the region; we saw Turks and Wallachs in battle, their swords dripping with bright, crimson arterial blood, the flickering shadows giving an illusion of movement to the gory tableau. One particularly gruesome scene depicted dozens of Turks writhing in the castle courtyard, all impaled on massive stakes, as the lords sat dining and watching them die. The image has lingered with me, par-ticularly since it appears the courtyard where the gipsies have pitched their camp is indeed the site of the charnel-house depicted on that tapestry.

Turning away, I examined the portraits that hung on one wall by the wide granite staircase, which led to darkened medieval hallways. Clearly, these men were all of the same lineage; strong men with aquiline noses, bushy dark hair when young, and receding hairlines when old. All had thick, shaggy eyebrows; most wore beards or mustaches, and none looked pleased to be sitting for their portraits.

I cast a look at my friend, who was just leaving the great hall to explore the other rooms. Holmes' own narrow, hawklike visage and widow's peak would not have been out of place in this family.

The Dracula wealth was in evidence everywhere. Dinner would be served on elaborate plates of gold, and the furniture, though centuries old, was exquisitely crafted, and I realized that much of it must have come as prizes of war from Turkey, perhaps even as far back as the Crusades. The portraits, landscapes and battle scenes amounted to a priceless art collection.

"No mirrors anywhere," Holmes said, returning from the hallway.

"Perhaps the Count is a vampire after all, Holmes. The lack of a reflection would give him away."

"My good fellow, there are no mirrors precisely because the Count does cast a reflection. How else to maintain the illusion?"

I nodded. All I wanted was to find Harker and head home.

"Well, there is no doubt now that Harker made it this far," he said, catching my gaze. "I've found Dracula's library. It's a bibliophile's dream, Watson. I only wish I could take a month to explore it. And the documents! Some of the Dracula papers are three hundred years old, and yet the handwriting on them is identical. What an odd family trait!"

"Or perhaps Dracula is deliberately imitating it to maintain the illusion of immortality," I said.

"Very good, Watson. Be that as it may, Dracula has been busy learning all things English. He's been studying the language, literature and history, but he doesn't seem too interested in current events. There are no English newspapers, and only a handful of magazines sent to him this year. The library also serves as his office, and in it I found Harker's address-book, some documents he brought with him, and return tickets."

"So Harker may still be here."

"We may hope, but the dates on those tickets passed weeks ago. The fact that they have not been used is most disturbing. We must conduct a search of the area."

As Holmes surmised, Harker's chamber was not far from the main hall. We found several octagonal chambers, each with a large bed, dressers, and sitting furniture, all as elaborate and old as that in the main hall. These, no doubt, were intended for the castle's tenants. Yet only Harker's was prepared for occupancy. The other rooms were old, dusty, and long disused.

"I think it's safe to say we should be searching for a burial site," Holmes said as we explored Harker's room. "His luggage, shaving-kit, clothing, stationery, are all here."

"There's a little blood on his razor," I noted.

"A few flecks, easily accounted for by a bad shave," Holmes replied. "You'll notice that Harker's shaving-glass is missing, too."

I tried the window. Locked.

"Holmes, isn't it possible that he simply made his way to the stable and stole a horse?"

Holmes shook his head.

"Had he done so, he certainly would have contacted Miss Murray. Have you tried the doors, Watson? Except for a stair to the floor above this one, anything leading to other parts of the castle is locked. I'm going upstairs now."

"Holmes," I asked, "where does Count Dracula sleep?"

"Certainly not on this floor," replied Holmes. "Come along."

The floor above was much like that adjacent to the great hall, but there were fewer suites on it. I thought they might be servants' quarters; some rooms had more than one bed, and they were smaller. Servants' quarters, but no sign of any servant.

This struck me as odd. Even if the Count lived alone, surely he would need at least a temporary maidservant to cook and clean while he was entertaining a guest. I've never heard of nobility making up a bed.

A cold rush of air from a window prompted me to summon Holmes.

"An open window! That is interesting," he said. Then his eyes widened, and he searched his pockets for his magnifying glass and measuring tape. Getting onto his knees, Holmes shuffled around the chamber performing the strange-looking ritual of measurement, grumbling and muttering the apparently random observations that cause so many to question his sanity. Yet no one can deny the results he achieves with it.

Several moments passed as he examined the window and its casement.

"Before I poke my head out, Watson, take a look at these marks in the dust. See those round depressions? A man's knee. The ovoid ones? Bootprints. The bootprints of a man tall enough to reach the casement with his knee, and desperate enough to believe this to be the way to freedom."

"Harker?"

"Who else?"

Holmes flung the window open wide, and I looked out on the dark Transylvanian valleys under the waning daylight and gathering clouds. A strong wind blew toward us and before long, it would be raining.

Leaning out, I saw a steep castle wall. The window opened to the south, and this part of the castle was built on a sheer rock face, down to the distant tree line below. As clouds darkened the sky, I saw bats flitting about, and heard the cries of wolves in the wind.

The terrain below the tree line was a thick, black forest, its dark mass broken by the rivers and tributaries that irrigate this land. Too far away for any but the most forlorn, the only sight of hope: the road to Bukovina, which looked like a piece of twine meandering through the hills.

"I don't like that wind, Holmes. Are you certain you wish to—"

He silenced me with a gesture. Now, glass in hand, Holmes leaned out.

"Hello! What's this?" he cried, and almost leaned too far. I pulled him back.

"This may be the route after all!" he cried. "Hold onto me! Take my legs!"

As Holmes dangled from the window, I had fearful visions of raindrops blinding me, of my grip slipping, of

Holmes vanishing with a scream into the trees, and my having to explain to his brother and to the world what it had lost in this remarkable man.

"Got it! Pull me up!"

My muscles were beginning to strain. I wanted to scold him for his carelessness, but was pleased that he trusted me so implicitly; as, indeed, would I trust him should I wish to do something so foolish.

But his face beamed with pleasure, and between his fingers was a single swatch of brown cloth.

"What does it mean, Holmes?"

"Harker, Watson! But he didn't plunge into the trees!"

"What do you mean?"

"There are handholds in the castle wall. Harker noticed them and used them to escape. Take a look at this cloth. Pure English-woven cotton, just like the trousers hanging in Harker's closet. Everyone here wears linen. No one else could have left this."

"Are you telling me he climbed a thousand feet down the castle wall, wandered down a steep mountain with no trail or guide, then made his way to the next town over?"

"No," said Holmes, "I am telling you that he climbed down one floor to the other open window and made his way out of the castle by safer means. Perhaps your theory about a stolen horse is correct, Watson. We are now beyond where the locked doors allow us to go from the main hall. Therefore, I think it probable that the window below us leads to the Count's chamber, or someplace near. Why else block it off? Provided Harker didn't fall, this is his likeliest escape route. Right now, take another look. Straight down."

I did. Sure enough, about fifteen feet below, was another window, also open.

"There's more," said Holmes. "Take a look at the stones beneath the windows. How far down can you see?"

"All the way."

"I'm talking about the holes in the wall."

Even with the roiling storm clouds moving in, I spotted them. Small holes were chipped out of the stone and appeared about every three feet beneath the windows.

"Hand- and toeholds at about the distance of a man's reach. I have to wonder what purpose they serve."

"Perhaps Count Dracula is a mountaineer."

"There would be pitons or some other way to use a rope, unless the Count is an extremely confident man. I expect the answer to this lies in the chamber below."

The storm came on us more rapidly than I expected, and a frosty gust blew into the window, which I closed.

"Not that way," I said. "Let's try to find some keys."

"We don't have time for this," Holmes said. "Harker is almost certainly dead. We have enough to make our sad report to Miss Murray. Let's go back to the library and see what we can learn there."

At first, we didn't learn much beyond the Count's travel plans. Holmes handed me a letter from Peter Hawkins, dated late in April:

"'I much regret that an attack of gout, from which malady I am a constant sufferer, forbids absolutely any travelling on my part for some time to come,'" it began.

"Miss Murray said nothing to us about an attack of gout," Holmes said. "She told us that Jonathan had been given an important assignment as a sign of confidence. Of course, it is possible Harker wanted to impress his fiancée and concealed the truth to improve his image in her eyes."

We also found correspondence to and from various shipping firms, and orders for a Russian ship called the *Demeter* to set sail from the Roumanian city of Varna. That ship left for England on 8 July.

"Harker had no doubt outlived his usefulness by then," said Holmes. "Ah, this should interest you. If we ever meet the Count, we'll have something to discuss."

Holmes handed me a copy of *Lippincott's Magazine*, which contained my account of the Sign of Four. The sight of the magazine twisted the knife in my heart; I was so absorbed in our adventure that, for the moment, I had put Mary out of my mind.

"You'll forgive me if I correct the more florid descriptions of how things happened," said Holmes.

"'Florid' also describes the state of your bank account since that story appeared," I snapped.

Holmes perceived that he had struck a nerve. "Touché," he replied softly. "Well, there are some financial documents in there that may prove interesting, and I'm not yet finished looking through the correspondence. You looked fatigued, dear fellow. Get some rest."

Holmes returned to the library for further researches, and I happily left him to it. Having found a *Lippincott's* I hadn't read, I settled into one of the fine carved wooden chairs by the fireplace, and I soon dozed, my bones weary, my heart agitated, but taking a cold pleasure that we had at least made progress.

Some hours later, I felt something like a small animal nuzzling my shoulder. Cracking open an eye, I saw for all the world what looked to be a white rat at my collar.

Startled, I leapt to my feet and slapped the creature down, only to see an equally startled Sherlock Holmes jump back, laughing.

"I'm sorry, Watson," he said, still laughing and offering me some of Dracula's brandy. "I thought you'd prefer to sleep in a proper bed, but first you should know that I've made a significant discovery."

"You found Harker stuffed into a bookcase," I said, somewhat embarrassed.

"Not quite. I've discovered instead a rather ingenious plot between the good professor and the mysterious count. I shall have to send a wire to Mycroft as soon as we reach civilization."

"What? Why?"

It took Holmes close to fifteen minutes to outline it for me, having a lot to do with international finance. I condense what I can remember from my somewhat misty memory:

"If you've got any money in overseas investments, Watson, pull it out now. Moriarty and Dracula are doing nothing less than engineering an international financial crisis. British banks have been loaning vast amounts of money to the Argentine government, which loans are guaranteed by said government. But the provinces and municipalities are borrowing heavily as well, and all there is to guarantee these loans is the word of the governments. The Argentine government, I have learned from conversations with my brother, is corrupt from top to bottom. There is no way these loans can be paid back; in fact, Moriarty has been bribing government officials to make sure of it. When the loans come due and there is no money, the banks will need help."

"Moriarty's?"

"Dracula's. We're sitting on a mountain of gold here, Watson, and over the past year or so, the count has been using Peter Hawkins as his agent to transfer his monies to accounts all over England—so much money that Dracula could be a bank unto himself. All it would take is for one of the larger loans to fail, a bank goes down with it, and in comes Dracula as the lender of last resort, giving him and Moriarty their very own bank in which to hide and legitimize any questionably acquired funds."*

"Do they have a particular bank in mind?"

"They do indeed—Baring Brothers. It's carrying the heaviest Argentine loans, and is the most vulnerable. Moriarty needs Dracula in England to immediately effectuate the necessary transfer of funds to rescue Barings when it collapses."

"What can your brother do about it?"

"Make sure that a legitimate bank steps in before Moriarty can make his move. I must say I admire their nerve, but we can't let them get away with it."

"I should check with my broker," I replied. "You don't suppose Dracula was really smuggling gold out in those earthen boxes, do you?"

"Unlikely," said Holmes, yawning. "Hawkins has dis-

---

* Holmes was right. In November 1890, the failure of the Buenos Aires Water Supply and Drainage loan of 1888 brought Barings down, but the Bank of England stepped in to salvage the disaster. By this time Dracula had been driven back to Transylvania (he died on Nov. 8), and Moriarty's greatest coup was thwarted. No wonder he felt "seriously inconvenienced" by Holmes. Presumably Moriarty had nothing to do with the 1995 crisis that destroyed Barings for good.

—SS

tributed Dracula's money into dozens of different invest-
ment accounts, trusts and annuities in different venues all
over England, so there's no need to have the gold physically
present. I have to wonder how much Harker knew of this."

By now it was quite late and Holmes looked positive-
ly cadaverish, so I administered immediate bed rest for us
both. We had a busy day on the morrow.

CHAPTER FOUR: MURDEROUS ATTACK UPON SHERLOCK HOLMES

Letter, Dr. Watson to Mary Watson

August 12, 1890
(Never sent)
Castle Dracula
Dear Mary,

If you receive this, it has been found on my body. I am dead. Please make arrangements not only for myself, but for the best friend to us both, Sherlock Holmes.

You must find Inspector Tobias Gregson in Scotland Yard and give him this letter. There may be mayhem afoot in London, particularly in the financial district.

You must also contact Miss Mina Murray, whose address appears at the end of this letter, and whose entreaties to Holmes sent us on this adventure. We have not found her fiancée, but I am willing to presume him dead—or worse.

As I write this, Holmes is deep in fever, and I fear may be dying. He has lost a great deal of blood, and we are alone, trapped in a mountain aerie in a foreign land. He is covered with wounds that don't seem to heal. He needs to be in hospital, but all he has is myself, my Gladstone bag, and the tools of medieval medicine. I am doing the best I can, but the sun is setting, and I fear the worst is to come.

We are sure of this: Jonathan Harker was a prisoner in Castle Dracula, and contrived to escape by climbing down the castle wall to a window that, in turn, led to egress from the castle.

I am all but certain Harker is dead. If not, then he has been driven mad and may have become an inhuman monster. In no circumstance will we have happy news for Miss Murray.

I do not mean to shock or dismay you. What follows is necessary for Inspector Gregson to do his duty. I must lay the facts out as I know them.

We hired gipsies to bring us to the castle, as none of the townspeople would do it, and they pitched camp in the castle's courtyard, promising to stay until we were ready to leave.

We awoke at dawn, as Holmes was eager to return to London, and I to you. But while we slept, a sudden snowstorm swept in, leaving several inches of cold, wet snow in the courtyard, with more coming down. We also discovered that the gipsies had abandoned us in the night. We were trapped at the castle with no means to leave, other than on foot in the middle of an icy gale.

"Watson!"

Holmes was in the stable. A small, shallow grave had been chipped out of the hard dirt floor. We retrieved shovels and exhumed the body. A small girl, no more than four years old, had been wrapped in a blanket and buried there. Her head had been cut from her tiny body, and her mouth stuffed with a garlic clove. This is how Roumanians deal with suspected vampires.

I confess that I started to weep, but Holmes forced me back to the business at hand.

"I know how you feel, Doctor, but perhaps there is

something else there. I need a trained medical eye if we are to achieve justice for this poor creature."

I steadied myself and set to work. At first, I could find nothing wrong, save for a touch of malnutrition. Properly cared for, she could have had a long, happy and fruitful life. Instead, she was sacrificed on the altar of vampire superstition.

But then I took a closer look at the severance point. It had been done cleanly, with a sharp blade. Just above the poor girl's collarbone, along the jugular vein, I found two punctures and the indentation of teeth. Probably human teeth; between the punctures I spotted a short, even scratch that no animal I know of would have left.

"This is sheer cruelty, Holmes," I said once I steadied myself. "It looks as though someone with extended canines tried to drink this girl's blood. Though that can't be possible. There are human monsters in the world, but none I know have fangs."

"We're not alone in this castle," Holmes said tensely.

"Could it have been Jonathan Harker?"

"I cannot dismiss the possibility," he said.

I fondled the crucifix that hung around my neck.

We fashioned a crude coffin from a feed bin, laid the poor child's remains in it and offered a prayer for her; the ground was too solid to dig even a shallow grave. Holmes nailed a note in German onto the lid asking whoever found it to give the girl a proper burial.

If only we had taken rooms overlooking the courtyard! We might have heard something and averted tragedy. With heavy hearts and little conversation, we made our toilets and breakfasted.

Holmes sank onto a sofa with his pipe and sat for

more than an hour, turning events and observations over in his mind. O, for a photographer! Sitting there by a fireplace the size of our sitting room, lost in contemplation, the smoke from the embers blending with the smoke from Holmes' own pipe, the very picture of quiet and determined ratiocination at work.

I shall always remember him thus, Mary. It is a pity I have only published two accounts of this admirable mind and keen intellect. They will no doubt sink into obscurity, and it will take the regular police years to learn that which comes to Holmes by instinct. And there is so much more to tell!

While Holmes was lost in the forest of analysis, I went back to the stable, in case there was anything to be found. I checked every window and door hoping for an open one, but no luck.

"You've been to the stable again, I perceive," Holmes said when I rejoined him. "Your boots attract straw like a magnet attracts nails."

"And keys," I said smugly, dangling a large ring thick with them, some hundreds of years old and some of recent manufacture.

"Watson! You outdo yourself! Where did you find them?"

"Hanging behind the door that led us into the castle in the first place."

Holmes smacked his forehead. "Well done," he said. "Now we can begin a true and proper search."

Mostly, we found unused, dusty rooms. But on the floor below our own, we found a stairway door that had been forced open and then fitted with a new lock. Holmes opened it with the shiniest key on the ring.

"Eureka!" he cried when the door swung open. "Harker has been here! Look!"

The floors had not been swept in centuries, and in the dust were three sets of footprints along the same general path. As I opened the windows to allow more light, Holmes examined the footprints in closer detail. Treading lightly along them with his glass, he followed them into several rooms, but eventually made a beeline toward the large suite that occupied the corner of the hallway. I tried the doors that had no footprints in front of them. Like so many of the others, they appeared to have been neglected since the 15th century or so.

I was standing in the smallest room we'd encountered so far; but for the furnishings and its place near the great hall, it was little more than a dungeon. Its tiny window looked out onto the courtyard, and I stared out. The temperature had risen slightly; the snow had turned to sleet, and now a thick crust of ice had formed on top of the snow. I had to remind myself it was still August.

The art fascinated me. The paintings here were unlike those in other parts of the castle. Though centuries old, the three pictures did not tell tales of conquest or extol the beauty of Transylvania. Something different was shown here.

The first painting depicted a wedding held in a chapel. The groom clearly hailed from the Dracula line, and the bride must have been a foreign noble; she wore bright red and green finery, and she had long, flowing blonde tresses, not often found in this region. I imagine in life she must have been quite beautiful. The groom's countenance is stern, the bride's apprehensive. It does not appear that the artist had any training or much natural ability;

Holmes agreed, when he saw the painting, that the style was close to primitive. I speculate that the artist may have been the only Dracula courtier available who could record the scene.

The second painting, executed by a surer hand, is a horror, showing demons claiming the bride's body as the helpless Dracula groom grovels to save her. From the dark buboes on her body and the bleeding wounds, I should say the poor woman died from plague. Yet the third painting, by the same artist, shows the demons bowing before Dracula's imperious glare as bodies blaze in a pyre—more evidence that plague swept through this castle.

Left unexplained is how that Dracula ancestor conquered the demons. Perhaps he caught the disease and somehow survived? It's rare, but not unheard of. A man who survived the plague might be seen as a demon in this part of the world.

I started when Holmes called my name from the door.

"Harker for sure," he said. "But a puzzle remains. It's all in the footprints."

I know this seems as though I'm rambling, Mary, but it is all important. For one thing, writing this is helping to soothe me as Holmes tosses and turns in his fever. My kingdom for a horse!

"Harker has walked these floors twice," said Sherlock Holmes. "This set of tracks represents his first time here, and he explored the rooms, but the large suite at the end of the hallway caught his attention. It is easy to see why; it has a writing-desk and grand views to the south and west. The set leading out is Harker returning to his room to avoid raising the Count's suspicions."

"There is only one more set, Holmes."

"Precisely, Watson. With the facts we have at hand, I believe that Harker tried to escape from that room. Come. We must investigate."

And so we did, for at least two hours. The views from that suite were as splendid as any of the others, but there were no handholds in the walls beneath them, as there are in other parts of the castle. If Harker had escaped by climbing down a wall, it was not this one.

All we knew for certain was that Jonathan Harker had been in that room and may have fallen asleep there; we could tell that from a large sofa that had been drawn into the room from a corner where it must have sat for two hundred years, and which had been dusted off. The dust in the casements was undisturbed. There was no other exit we could find, and there was nothing whatsoever to indicate by what means he had left the room.

"Curious, Watson," Holmes finally admitted. "I cannot explain it."

"Let us locate Count Dracula's chambers," I said. "We'll find answers there."

We took a look out the southern window for a fresh calculation of where the Count's room was likely to be and walked down the cold stone stairway. If we were looking for a family crest or other sign of nobility to identify the door, then we were disappointed. Holmes singled out a thick anonymous oak door as the one; it could have as easily been a storeroom. It didn't seem to have been opened for years.

"Are you sure, Holmes?"

He replied by placing a key in the rusty lock. It took all Holmes' considerable strength to turn the tumblers, and both our shoulders were needed to push the door open. Save for some old furniture and a great pile of coins on the floor, the room was empty.

Holmes was frankly shocked.

"This can't be," he said, and then his face relaxed; there was another door in the room. "Another stairwell, Watson."

"Take a look at these coins, Holmes," I said. "Some of these guineas go back to Henry VIII. There's old Greek money here, Turkish, German ... a numismatist would be in heaven. I can't begin to imagine what they're worth in sterling."

"The Count must be a trusting man," Holmes said. "Perhaps he used this room to mask the true location of his chamber. We'd better get lanterns."

Down the chilly, damp spiral staircase we went. After groping our way for what seemed like hours, we reached the bottom and the rich, unmistakable aroma of moldy earth. We followed the aroma down another dark, dank passage that eventually led to the ruins of a medieval chapel.

What magnificence lost to history! Gaping holes in the roof allowed the elements to ravage what must centuries ago have been a thriving and devout house of worship. Indeed, we had to elude bullets of sleet as we made our way about. Massive curtains and shutters blocked the elaborate stained glass windows that once glowed with the passion of Christ. There was more family history, with elaborate carved panels of Dracula heroics in the Crusades adorning the sanctuary. The wood was rotten in some areas, and centuries of wind, rain and snow caused some of the panels to splinter.

Once we opened some of the windows, we could see

that, a long time ago, a great deal of vandalism had been committed. All relics of the Catholic Church had been eradicated. The altar was demolished, and the accoutrements of worship—candlesticks, goblets, vestments, Bibles—all were gone. Once the afternoon's dull grey light filled the room, I could see that the carved panels served a double purpose; they covered up any sacramental art that might be on the walls.

The room began to darken again, and the sleet fell harder.

"The vaults have to be nearby," said Holmes.

The first two we encountered held nothing of interest, except to an archaeologist. But the third, a vast cavern easily the size of the great hall, showed signs of much recent excavation. So much earth had been dug up that the workmen might have been laying a new foundation.

Holmes sighed. "This is where the gipsies dug the earth the Count wanted shipped to England," he said. "If Harker is still here, then this is the likeliest place we'll find his body. Let's see if anything looks like a fresh grave."

Despite the cold and sleet, we opened several windows to let in the feeble light. Our searches were painstaking and thorough, and at the end of them, we found nothing except indentations where some large coffin-sized boxes had been piled.

"You don't suppose Dracula shipped the body out in one of the boxes for later disposal, do you?" I suggested.

"That's precisely what I think. A box that heavy would never surface, especially if it were dropped in fresh water along the way."

In the end, our searches proved fruitless. All that digging, and nothing to show for it; certainly nothing to point us in the direction of Jonathan Harker. We returned to the great hall and lit a fire.

Later. Fool that I am, I fell asleep for nearly an hour. Holmes is worse, and now I truly despair for his life. Luckily, the storm drove some of the chickens the gipsies left behind into the stable for shelter, and I have butchered one. What an unanticipated use for my surgical talents! It will soon be done roasting. I plan to pack some of the meat for a journey down the mountain, and will make some chicken broth with the carcass. That should boost Holmes' strength if he can keep it down.

Right now, his head is bright with fever, and his rantings tell me he is experiencing horrific nightmares; indeed, perhaps he is going through last night all over again.

I don't feel very well myself. The altitude and the cold have been playing havoc with my war wounds, and my shoulder is singing with pain right now.

To the business at hand. The storm eventually subsided, and cold, clear moonlight streamed through the windows, providing the only light in the hallways. I spent a good part of the evening in the library updating my journal (which I also want you to give to Inspector Gregson) while Holmes found an ancient tub and heated some water for a soaking bath.

I had the strangest hallucination as I walked down the hallway to my room. There were motes of dust dancing in the moonlight. I know there is nothing unusual about that, but these seemed to be forming into something. As they moved, they drew closer together. I could not break my gaze; there was a mesmerizing quality to the sight.

And then I saw three women materialize out of the darkness.

Please know that what I write now is not written to hurt you, despite our recent difficulties; but I cannot omit these events, and I will not lie to you.

So captivated was I by the dancing dust that I did not see the women step into the soft white moonlight. I can only describe them as gorgeous, the essence of feminine beauty made alabaster flesh. All I could see at first were their smiles, sharp white teeth dazzling in the moon's rays, their tresses flying free, their garments white, loose and flowing.

In the back of my mind I thought of that poor gipsy girl and the sharp bite marks on her neck, but that image faded as the women drew closer to me.

Did they not notice the cold? I wondered absurdly.

Two of these sirens might have been fraternal twins and were almost certainly members of the Dracula family. The sharp, stark features that made the Dracula men so forbidding gave these women frosty, regal beauty. To see that stern visage and high forehead softened and made lovely in feminine form both disquieted me and drew me ever closer. Their lips were full, red and voluptuous, and their eyes seemed to glow like red coals in the darkness.

The third, clearly their leader, was more slender, but also more striking, with hair like spun gold flying about, and an unmistakable sense of familiarity stole over me as I struggled to remember where I had seen her before.

She said something in Hungarian, and then it struck me like a thunderbolt. *She was the very image of the Dracula wife who had died of plague centuries before!*

She said something else in Hungarian. I stared, mute as a post, and then one of them said, her voice mellifluous and seductive despite her accent, "Are you the English also?"

I nodded dumbly.

"You stare with such wonder," she said. "Have you never seen women before?"

"I thought I had," I replied, almost in a whisper.

I should have run away but I could not. Despite their demeanour, their luminosity, their increasingly obvious hunger, I felt myself slipping into a soporific state. I could not have stopped them from working their will even if the castle had been burning down around my ears.

I took a step forward, and remembered the crucifix given to me by the village innkeeper. Frantically, I thrust it at them.

The women hissed like cats and shied away as if blinded by a flash. I found strength to hold the icon up and then, down the hall, a door opened. Sherlock Holmes emerged from his bath, clad only in his dressing-gown.

"Holmes!" I cried. "Run! They killed Harker!"

A harsh silvery laugh greeted my sally. The women passed me swiftly and attacked Holmes, shoving him into his room and slamming the door. I heard the lock snap, and groaned; Holmes had the keyring. Inside I heard harsh, crystalline laughter, and thought of what cats must feel on capturing a sparrow.

You know well Holmes' indifference to the charms of the fairer sex, but from the lascivious sounds from behind the door, I could tell he was succumbing. I heard no resistance.

I pounded on the door and bellowed.

"Your crucifix! Holmes, the crucifix!"

More laughter, some frightening sounds of struggle, and then soft murmuring and soon, silence.

Had I been thinking clearly, I would have gone to the

woodshed and returned with an axe. But bloody images of what they were doing to Holmes filled my head, and I became a crazed man.

That's when I remembered the south window. If there were handholds for one room, there must be for others. I raced upstairs, to the room above Holmes'. I whipped the window open and a pale yellow beam filled the space, a cold breeze blowing in.

Looking down, there were handholds, unless they were shadowy illusions of the moonlight. Thinking of the horrid fate even now befalling my closest friend, I tentatively dipped a toe to the first hold. It slid in smoothly. I lowered myself to my full body length. Another toehold, then a handhold. The chilly breeze frayed my face as I groped in the shadows, and the castle's stone was rough and mocking as I held my cheek to it, not daring to look down.

Thick, dark clouds blotted the moon. My light vanished, and the breeze became a chilly wind, numbing my face, my fingers, and my sense of touch.

Gingerly now, I found another handhold, another toehold. My foot slipped once and I cried out, but I did not fall. Another step, and then another. Two bats flitted by and seemed to be circling me, waiting for a mistake. They came uncomfortably close and I stopped moving, hoping they would go away.

By now, I could hear the sounds from Holmes' open window more clearly. A cold steady rain began to fall, which was a mixed blessing. Soon I would not be able to feel my fingers at all, but my presence would be harder to detect. Hard droplets pricked my face.

"Please. You must be sated by now," Holmes said in a soft, pleading voice.

"It's been so long, *Englisch*," said one of the women, and I heard a weak whimper from Holmes. "That child was barely enough, and the Count has abandoned us."

"If we are greedy tonight, then it might be a long time until our next opportunity," said another. "And the other one is still loose."

More chilling laughter.

I almost fell again when I put my foot to what I thought was a toehold and connected with air. The window!

It took long, agonizing minutes in the icy rain to steel myself for what I had to do. By now I could no longer feel my hands nor trust my frozen fingers. But I leaned as far as I could to my right, my war-wounded shoulder a symphony of pain, and groped along rough, bitter stone for a solid hand-hold even as my mind pictured over and over again my plunge to certain death on the rocks far below if my unfeeling fingers failed me. I squeezed both my hands into the tiny hole, champed my lip, and kicked free.

My lower back clipped the casement as I swung into the room, and then I cracked the back of my head as I landed, but the harpies were too surprised to do anything but react. I clumsily thrust my crucifix at them as stars danced on the edges of my vision.

The ghastly sight will be with me to my dying day. Holmes lay on the bed, impotent and semi-conscious. The women were arrayed around him like vultures dividing up prey. Fresh, bright arterial blood dripped from the harpies' lips, and one was sucking at a fresh wound opened on Holmes' chest when I landed.

I faced the blonde, who was leaning over Holmes when she saw me. She had exposed her breast, which was bleeding freely, and when I saw the dark spots around

Holmes' mouth, I realized with a shock that she had made him drink, too.

They hissed and stepped around the bed, acting as a barricade as I pulled my body in through the window.

"Begone!" I barked, waving my crucifix. The women shrieked. Cold and in pain, I struggled to get to my feet.

The women were gone as suddenly as they had come. I was in such pain that I did not hear the door or even see them leave. I had a more pressing concern.

I lit candles and gasped in horror. Nearly naked, Holmes' pale white body was covered with several deep wounds. He had been bitten at the jugular vein, which now flowed freely, as did fresh bites to his breast, near his heart, and the harpies had also punctured the carotid artery at Holmes' neck. It did not seem humanly possible to lose so much blood so quickly.

Luckily, the jugular wound looked worse than it actually was. There were only two small puncture marks, and these I was able to seal with plaster from Holmes' shaving kit. The arterial wound required stitching. Securing my crucifix around Holmes' neck, I left long enough to get my Gladstone and some wet towels for a cold compress.

Some of the other wounds were more problematic. They were close to the heart, and looked deep. If the bleeding wasn't stopped soon, Holmes would be dead.

"My dear Holmes," I said in my most reassuring, doctorly manner. "It's I. It's Watson. Come on now, old boy. Open your eyes if you can."

"W— Wat—"

He tried to raise his head, but it sank back into the pillow.

"No, no, not yet, Holmes."

I applied a cold towel to the chest wounds and pressed; it was all I had. Warm, dark stains soon appeared. I applied another, and then another. It seemed like hours later, but the bleeding finally stopped and I closed the wounds with stitches.

I lifted one of his eyelids and brought a candle close. The pupil responded as it should; at least there was no obvious brain damage. Lifting his thin, pale and deathly white hand, I held the flame under his palm, and that did it. He snapped awake and snatched his hand away.

"Watson!" he said, and coughed. After several minutes he said softly, "It's a wonder you retain any patients at all with a bedside manner like that."

"What happened, Holmes?"

"Did I not dream it?" he asked, his voice feeble. "It's hard to know. My memory is dissipating like the morning fog. I found three women in here as I returned from my bath. I can't really describe them except to say they were the most beautiful, alluring creatures I have ever seen. You know me, Watson. I have never fully trusted the sex; even the best of them gives me pause. But these ..."

His eyes started to close.

"Not yet, Holmes," I said slapping him gently. "Try to stay awake while I find some brandy."

By the time I returned from the wine cellar, it was too late. He had fallen back on the bed, unconscious.

We've been here ever since. Holmes has been going in and out of delirium, his ravings both fascinating and ter-rifying. Even more baffling and disquieting is a new symp-tom I have never seen before: Holmes' canines are growing and have become noticeably sharper. Outside of vampire superstition, I can't explain it.*

I have found two other crucifixes; one is in the window, and the other is over Holmes' bed. I haven't slept, except for a few fitful turns during the day.

I find that two hours have passed since I began to write, and that I am almost out of paper. I have found a suitably sized envelope in the Count's office, and I am addressing it to you, Mary, in the hope it will find its way to you some day. Know that, in this life and in the next one, that you are ever dear to my heart, that I love you now and will love you until the twilight of time.

Your adoring husband,
John

---

* The University of Michigan may have found a way. According to *Science Daily,* (Feb 12, 2005) researchers mixed bone morphogenetic proteins with an inactive virus and injected it into rats needing dental implants. The rats grew back much of the bone needed to support the implants. A Kirkland, Wash. company called Dentigenix is using this and other research to pursue the regrowth of human teeth using the body's own cells. —SS

CHAPTER FIVE: ESCAPE FROM CASTLE DRACULA

Letter, Dr. Watson to Mary Watson

August 20, 1890
Kimpelung, Bukovina
Dear Mary,

I apologise for not writing sooner, but Holmes fell ill while we were at Castle Dracula. The gipsy band we hired for transportation and assistance abandoned us, a sudden snowstorm trapped us, and we had little choice but to wait until the road was clear. This trip has not been a holiday, believe me.

On top of that, we never found Jonathan Harker. Holmes thinks it likely, and I concur, that he fell from a high window. It would require a team of skilled mountaineers to search the area for his body, and neither of us is fit nor equipped for such a task.

I expect to see you Sunday or Monday. And what a story I shall have to tell.

> Your ever loving husband,
> John

*　　*　　*

Dr. Watson's Journal

August 20, 1890
Safe at last.

Holmes and I are in a small, quaint hotel in Kimpelung, Bukovina. How I have missed the bustle of humanity! We are in the center of town on a warm summer's eve. The windows are open, and the sounds of conversation in the street, of commerce being conducted, the clip-clop of horses' hooves are like a symphony to me after the harsh isolation of Castle Dracula.

Holmes' fever broke last Friday, giving me some hope that we would soon leave Dracula's horrid citadel.

"Poor Watson!" Holmes whispered as I gave him water. "You haven't slept for days. Will you ever forgive me for bringing you on this hopeless quest?"

"Quiet, dear fellow," I told him. "There is nothing to forgive."

"Those women—"

"Gone, or in hiding."

"I had dreams. They were at the window …"

I had placed a crucifix at every entrance to Holmes' room, as well as one around his neck. It seemed to have great power over the women, though such a thing has never turned up in any vampire tales I've ever read. In any event, the women haven't returned since the attack. Our only company in the castle was a handful of bats flocking by Holmes' window.

"We have to leave," said Holmes.

"Can you get up?"

Holmes nodded. It was a bit of a struggle, as he had not left his bed in days, but once he was on his feet, I knew the worst was truly over. His wounds are healing more rapidly than I have any right to expect. Perhaps it's the chicken soup.

But, in all my medical experience, in war, across three

continents, I have never encountered what is happening with Holmes' teeth. His frightening sharp canines have fallen out, and are being replaced by teeth of normal length and evenness. This phenomenon is unknown to me. I'll keep this knowledge to myself for the time being; there may be something in the literature to explain it.

Reading over the letter I wrote to Mary, I realize I must have been delirious myself. There are perfectly rational, logical and scientific reasons for what happened, even if I don't know what they are right now. Vampires do not exist outside the imaginations of Dr. Polidori or Mr. LeFanu.

That these women believe themselves to be vampires, I have no doubt; why else would Dracula keep them about? They share the same superstitions that grip the minds of the villagers, and we are in the land that gave us the Countess Elisabeth Bathory, who bathed in the blood of young girls in hopes of preserving her own youth. Perhaps Dracula's women share the Countess' belief that the drinking of blood grants eternal youth and beauty. I wish I had paid better attention to which hallway they came from. Unless there are still more secret chambers in that castle. I thank God that I will never return to it!

Holmes and I discussed the nature of vampirism at length as we waited for the snow to melt.

"There is simply no way I can accept vampire superstition," Holmes said. "These people are masters of illusion, nothing more."

"How do you explain it, then?"

"Count Dracula is a mystic, perhaps a devil worshiper, and he leads a vampire cult. Everything we've seen here supports it: the lack of mirrors, the banning of Christian imagery, the blood rituals."

"How do you explain your symptoms?"

"Poison, injected through the skin. They get away with it by exploiting local superstitions, reinforcing the superstitions with their terrifying actions, and enough stagecraft and chemical trickery to hold the belief of gullible minds. I shall not give in to it."

"How do you explain the teeth?" I asked. "There is no mention of growth like that in any of the literature I know of, medical or otherwise."

"I admit that I haven't worked it all out yet," Holmes said. "Dracula has possibly included some folk chemical in his poison that science has yet to explain. I emphasize 'yet,' Watson."

"Perhaps the women truly believe in the power of Christ," I said. "Perhaps those crosses are keeping them away."

For whatever reason, the women did not approach us again, and I did not try to find them. Sherlock Holmes was my sole concern. Once I was able to apply the medical knowledge of this century, he improved rapidly. By Sunday, the snow had receded enough to allow us to leave.

"At least we'll be walking downhill," he said. "Your leg should be able to stand it, I trust?"

We left at dawn, taking a healthy heap of the Count's gold coins as compensation for our travails. I kept looking over my shoulder until the castle was no longer in sight, but I didn't feel truly safe until we were beyond the melting snow and under the cover of the trees.

We reached the main road at nearly four o'clock in the afternoon. Between my aching shoulder and stiff leg, and Holmes' weakness, we were obliged to rest every twenty minutes or so.

We struck east; neither one of us wanted to risk the village and take the blame in case more children had disappeared. The evening coach came by about two and a half hours later, as the sky was beginning to redden with twilight.

I took a look back up at the castle, now many miles away atop a distant mountain. Clouds drifted along the battlements. Even far away and small, the castle looked stark and forbidding, and the red sunlight glowing on it made me think of all the blood spilled in its lengthy and splendid history. Again I thought of Holmes' ordeal, and felt a chill.

Then we rounded a bend, and that is the last I ever hope to see of Castle Dracula.

PART TWO

THE PLAGUE OF DRACULA

CHAPTER SIX: COUNT DRACULA

Dr. Watson's Journal

August 27, 1890

My wife has gone missing, and I don't know what to do.

It seems that my darkest fears have been realized. I never expected a warm welcome, and now I fear that this Transylvanian trip has sealed my fate. Rather than my absence making Mary's heart grow fonder, she has chosen to wander instead. My marriage is over.

Mary and the serving-girl seem to have vanished. Significantly, Mary's luggage is missing, but it is unlike her not to leave a note. I have sent a wire to Mrs. Cecil Forrester, that good lady who brought us together. But in case there is evidence here I might unwittingly disturb, I have decided to spend the night at Baker Street and discuss the whole matter with Holmes.

Later. I am back home. Mrs. Hudson informed me that Holmes left for, of all places, Whitby, almost immediately upon his arrival. I am at a loss. I feel paralyzed without Holmes' guidance. I shall wire everyone Mary could possibly be with and await answers. If there are none by the end of my morning rounds, then it's off to Scotland Yard.

August 29, 1890

After an agonizing, restless night, I returned to Baker Street in the hope of catching Sherlock Holmes, but found a surprise instead.

Among the letters to Holmes in this morning's post was one I hadn't expected to see—from Mrs. Cecil Forrester. I opened it without shame, but with great heartache. It read:

Winchester, the Pentangeli
August 24, 1890
My dear Mr. Sherlock Holmes,
I need both your tact and your discretion this hour. I am breaking a confidence in writing to you. Mrs. Watson has decided to leave her husband. You are the cause, I'm afraid: it is Mary's belief that Dr. Watson far prefers your company to hers, and she has been trysting with another man, whose name I do not know, but who I believe is causing her great distress.

Mary came to me Wednesday, on the 20th. She was unhappy and withdrawn, and told me she was visiting for clear country air. But during one sleepless night, I rose for tea and saw her, in her night clothes, wandering across the lawn. I called to her, but she did not seem to hear. Instead, she made her way to the gazebo by the lake. Waiting for her was a tall, elegant man, of strong bearing and noble features, in evening dress, possibly a foreigner. Mary took his hand and he absorbed her in his arms in a passionate embrace. I returned to the house immediately.

In the morning, I confronted her, and

she confessed. But I believe she truly pines yet for the arms of her husband. Since her arrival she shows all the signs of a broken heart. Mary has grown pale and gaunt, and refuses to eat. But she also refuses to let me get in touch with Dr. Watson, saying she will do so when she feels the time is ripe.

And so, Mr. Holmes, once again I turn to you. I am in hopes that you can resolve the situation one way or another, for while I am loath to harbor an adulteress, you know how dear Mary is to me. You have spared me heartache in the past, Mr. Holmes, and I implore you to do it again.

Yours most sincerely,

Mrs. Cecil Forrester

My own heart is aflame with rage, and pain, and pity. Have I so neglected my wife? Since our marriage, weeks have often passed without my seeing Holmes. True, I have accompanied him on a number of cases, but rarely have these exceeded one or two nights, and for the ones in London I usually slept at home. Mary always seemed to delight in the stories of our doings.

I am now torn. Honour binds me to pretend I never saw this letter that was not meant for my eyes, but how can I bear to lose a wife for the second time? And who is this strange lover? I must speak with Holmes! Why doesn't he answer?

September 1, 1890

Tonight, the ashen tastes of defeat and disappointment lie heavy on my heart, not to be dispelled by any amount of brandy. For Sherlock Holmes has brought Mary back to me, it is true, but at the highest price. She does not know me, and does not want me.

After I read Mrs. Forrester's letter, I packed a valise and caught the next train south to Winchester, knowing I was going to do something, but completely bamboozled exactly as to what it was I wanted to do. My initial rage subsided as the clacking tracks lulled me to the first deep sleep I'd had since our return. I dreamt heavy, poisonous dreams, murderous dreams in which I throttled the mystery Lothario and swept my Mary back into my arms. I also had dreams in which I throttled her, but always stopped myself at the last. Once or twice I vividly felt Holmes' touch on my arm, but when I opened my eyes I was alone.

The naps purged my rage, and when I woke my mind was somewhat clear. I decided to broach the matter with Mary in my best professional manner, and diagnose whether our heartbreak could be cured. If not, I was prepared to offer generous terms for divorce and move back to Baker Street.

Mrs. Forrester and her retinue live at the Pentangli, or the Five Angels, the estate purchased by the late Colonel Forrester on his retirement from military service. There are still remnants of the ancient Roman stronghold the area once was, when Winchester was the capital; the rocky remains of a storehouse can be found on one shore of the lake, and Forrester incorporated the ruins of the battlements when he constructed the estate's exterior walls. Happily, the gate was open as my cab brought me up the long white gravel drive to the front of the mansion.

My hand, cold and colourless, trembled as I reached

for the brass knocker on the Pentangeli's heavy oaken door, and I almost went back to London. But the cab had left, and there was nothing for it but to go ahead. I presented my card to the butler and waited.

Mrs. Cecil Forrester, a stout lady whose iron-gray coiffure and haughty demeanour mask a heart of gold, came to the door herself.

"Doctor Watson!" she ejaculated. "Whatever are you doing here?"

"You didn't answer my wire," said I, "so I came to inquire in person if you know where Mary might be."

"Oh, dear, I'm not sure if I should tell you." Then she blushed.

"May I see her, please?"

"Truthfully, Doctor, I think you must! She's fallen dreadfully ill. She's lost a great deal of weight in the last week, takes naught but broth, and wanders in the night. But she refuses any medical attention."

"Take me to her!"

A powerful air of impending death filled Mary's sickroom. A slight woman to begin with, she had lost at least fifteen pounds since last I saw her. She had the pallor of a corpse, and her breathing was shallow. Her nightdress was buttoned right up to her chin, and long, unkempt blonde hair spilled over her pillows with indifference; but when she saw me her eyes, a harsh, unnatural yellow, blazed with hatred.

"Get out!" she spat, and I noticed that her canines were already sharper. My stomach clenched.

"You're ill, my dear," I said as soothingly as I could. "Let's not discuss our difficulties right now. We can do that after we go home."

"I have no home with you!" she snapped. "Your home's with Holmes! All he has to do is wave his hat and off you run to adventures with royalty, and Scotland Yard! And why must all your readers write to you? We're drowning in correspondence! I can't take it anymore, and now I won't!"

The penny finally dropped and I knew what had happened. I snatched at Mary's collar, exposing two horrid bite marks on my wife's jugular. The same bite marks I had seen on Holmes and that poor gipsy girl; red, raw, and oozing black venous blood.

"Who is he?" I snapped. "Count Dracula?"

Her sharp intake of breath told me all. I sat down on the bed as she shied away.

"You can't keep me from him!" Mary cried. "He loves me! He was here when I needed him! Where were you?"

I rang the bell, and two servant girls answered.

"I am Doctor John Watson, and this is my wife, Mary," I said. "Mrs. Watson is extremely ill, and must be removed from this house at once. Get a carriage and some strong hands. We are going to London."

"No!"

Mary's hand lashed out and caught my right cheek by the eye. Howling, I snatched her hand away, and she dashed from the room.

"After her!" I yelled, and ran out the door.

But she was too quick. Blood dripped into my eye, and I tripped on the carpet, sprawling on my face. I heard a door slam, and the last anyone saw of Mary she had flown into the woods.

"Doctor Watson, I'm so sorry!" Mrs. Forrester said as

she leaned over me, dabbing at my dripping wound with her handkerchief. "What will become of the poor girl?"

"Have your staff search the woods, if you please," I said. "She's lost a lot of blood. She won't go far in her condition."

But the searches proved fruitless. After plastering my scratches (the wound to my pride was far deeper), I decided to do what Holmes would do. Her trysting place with the Count was the gazebo by the trout pond, and it was likely he would meet with Mary there. I borrowed a shotgun and shells from the trophy room, found a suitable spot behind a lakeside boulder at sunset, and began my vigil.

A bright half moon rose in the sky, casting a pale yellow glow over the undulating waters. Several tempting ducks waddled by for their evening feed, but I needed my shells for darker things. The twilight waned; no sign of the Count, or of Mary. Mist formed on the placid pond, thickening into fog. Soon, I could only see the gazebo's outline with any sort of clarity. Still I waited.

At least two more hours must have passed before I saw a tall, slender, aquiline figure who could only be Count Dracula silhouetted in the fog. He moved with great purpose across the grounds toward the gazebo. He surveyed the scene carefully, as if he knew I was there. He peered behind bushes and walked toward the trees, before finally taking his place.

As he stood, another figure approached: Mary, cold and sallow, still in her thin white nightdress, moving hesitantly, clumsily across the slippery grass. I aimed the shotgun carefully. This was not a pistol; if my finger were not sure, I might harm my wife, and bad as things were, I could never want that. The fog seemed to thicken as I cocked the shotgun as quietly as I could.

The tall man snapped his head up and yelled "Watson!" just as I pulled the trigger.

A mighty blast went into the air, for I recognized the voice in time. Mary screamed and disappeared into the dank fog.

"You fool!" cried Holmes as he ran to me. "You romantic, blithering fool! You just cost us everything!"

"Not so, Mr. Sherlock Holmes," said another voice, heavy with the syllables of Roumania and as frightening as the shadow of death. "I believe we have some business."

Seemingly from nowhere appeared a tall, gaunt man, aged no more than thirty, with a long black moustache and dressed entirely, and elegantly, in black. His thick black hair was swept back in a regal manner, and his breath reeked of decay. Though I could not see his face clearly, the glittering twin red coals that served as his eyes fixed on me, and I shuddered as an icy finger, it seemed, ran the length of my spine. There was no doubt in my mind that we had, at last, met Count Dracula.

"And Doctor Watson has joined us!" said the Count. "I have heard a great deal about you lately, Doctor."

I popped the shotgun open to replace the spent shell, but I heard a low growling and saw five grey wolves with blazing red eyes trotting toward the Count from the woods. They sat around him in a circle, poised to pounce, and never took their gaze away from us.

"I congratulate you, Mr. Holmes," said the Count.

"I know all," Holmes replied. "I know about your bargain with Professor Moriarty and your plans for Barings Bank. I know why you are in London. I know how you eluded the authorities. You cannot succeed. If I can find you, so can others."

"They have not your admirable tracking skills," said the Count. "But I am no longer beholden to Moriarty. It is not my fault you escaped at the castle; honour is satisfied. Now I think we can come to a mutually beneficial agreement."

"I will hear what you have to say."

"It is rumoured that you have little use for the fair sex," Dracula said, stepping closer. "Does that include Mary Watson?"

As he said this, two of the wolves padded over to Mary, who swayed in the moonlight, barely able to stand. My fingers atremble, I tried to reload the shotgun, dropping two spare shells before success. When the weapon clicked shut, a wolf bared its fangs and squatted on its haunches, ready to spring.

"I will not allow you to kill her." Holmes started to pull a crucifix from his vest, but a growl from two of the wolves stopped him.

"For five hundred years, your kind has hounded me with cross and stake, garlic and fire," Dracula said. "You think you can beat me. I say to you that you will never beat me. Still I stand, as I will long after your bones blow away in the dusty wind. You will not harm me unless you wish Mary Watson to become one with me. Put your toys away. I am a reasonable man."

I raised the shotgun, but again Holmes stopped me.

"I will release her," Dracula said, "but in return you must drop your pursuit."

"Nothing you could say will sway me from my course."

The wolves began to sniff my terrified wife. I started to go to her, when the beast which had been eyeing me leapt, gripping my forearm in its terrible jaws. Barking with the sudden pain, I dropped the shotgun. Blood spurted from my arm, distracting the Count.

Holmes sprang, but a wolf blocked him and sank its teeth into his shoulder, thrashing its head to and fro, worrying Holmes into submission. He cried out, but shifted his weight suddenly and pulled free, tearing cloth and flesh, spurting blood, and coming toward me. Scooping the shotgun from the ground, he brought the butt down hard on the angry beast's head.

A cruel, sharp laugh cut the air. When I looked at Mary, the Count had taken her in his arms, and with a fiendish grin at me, lowered his lips to her wounded neck.

The shotgun thundered and the wolf who attacked Holmes yowled and ran away. The others turned their attention to him, but Holmes' eye was only on the Count. Holmes had scant seconds to get off the second shot before the other wolves jumped him.

"No!" I cried. "Count Dracula! If we let you go, will Mary recover fully?"

Dracula's grin was odious with victory. He gestured, and the remaining wolves sat, their growls low and steady. "I shall release her from the spell. I will not taste her again."

"Holmes—"

But he held the shotgun steady.

"This is my wife, Holmes! My wife!"

The Count stood silently, imperiously. So lost was I in anger and rage and impotence, it seemed to me that he was floating above the ground. A wolf padded over and sat next to his right hand. It bared its sharp yellow fangs in a threatening snarl. The hair on my neck bristled, and my heart beat loudly and rapidly in my ears.

"If you ever loved me, Holmes ..." I pleaded.

With reluctance, Holmes lowered the shotgun and pressed his free hand against his wound.

"Let not our paths cross again," said the Count, "or the consequences will be dire."

Now I wept openly, and I should probably be grateful that I could not discern Holmes' face in the darkness.

"May the Lord God help you if they do," Holmes replied.

I did not see the Count or his wolves leave, so joyous was my relief. The fog began to dissipate, and soon the moonlight again glinted off the pond. In the gazebo, I saw a gaunt, yet lovely, blonde form slumped over on one of the benches.

"Brandy, Holmes!"

He wordlessly handed his flask over. Ignoring my own pain, I tilted my beloved's head back, gently pried her mouth open, and poured the life-giving liquor down her fragile throat.

Mary coughed and sputtered, but took in deep, healthy breaths.

"John?" she asked, a little confused. "Mr. Holmes? What are you doing here?"

"You've been ill, my darling," I told her. "You came to Mrs. Forrester to recover in the fresh air. You're going to be all right."

Holmes nodded softly with encouragement, but said nothing. He had slumped against a bench, his hand pressed to his shoulder, staining the white woodwork with his dark blood.

"You need rest now, Mary," I said. "We go home in the morning."

"I miss London," she said, yawned, and passed out.

"I demand an explanation," said I to Holmes.

"Not now."

I tore off my sleeve and bound Holmes' wound to stop the bleeding for now; the wolf's bite went deep and there would be considerable scarring. His left arm would be almost useless for at least a week; my other sleeve served as a temporary sling. Silent and sullen, he limped behind me as I carried Mary back to the mansion.

I prepared Mary's chamber by placing crucifixes on every wall and wreaths of garlic at every entrance to the room, dithering about the comfort of Christ and the amazing healing powers of garlic. I told Mrs. Forrester to have Mary ready to leave by early afternoon the following day.

Holmes and I went to a nearby pub, where we shared our thoughts over beer and cigars.

"What were you doing there?" I asked him.

"Tracking Count Dracula, as should have been obvious," he replied. "If you had bothered to read the newspapers that piled up when we were away, it would not have escaped your attention that the *Demeter's* hulk washed up on the shores of Whitby. A sight of genuine horror, Watson. The crew dead or missing, a large wolf apparently responsible for many of the deaths, the captain's body lashed to the wheel, the very essence of fear stamped on his face at the end.

"Unfortunately, by the time I got there the Russian government had taken control of the wreck and wouldn't let anyone near it, with one exception: the workmen whose job it was to remove the fifty boxes of earth being imported to England by Count Dracula.

"I saw the hand of Professor Moriarty in this right away, and as usual no direct proof that he was involved. The boxes have been taken to Dracula's estate in London, as far as I know. I suppose I'll find out tomorrow."

"You almost sacrificed Mary," I said.

"I would not have, my dear Watson. I am an excellent shot; the Count's body would have taken the blast, and put an end to this vampire nonsense once and for all."

"Will you still go after him?"

"Of course. How many deaths is he responsible for? How much madness? And what is yet to come? We must hunt him down."

I was on the edge of tears. How could he be so callous? Does justice mean so much? Whatever instilled this blinding passion in the man? Close as we are, I know so little of his life before he came to London.

"Please don't, Holmes. I can't risk Mary again. Turn it over to Gregson."

"What?"

"You heard me, Holmes. I almost lost my wife tonight, and cannot bear to chance it again. Where was Gregson when he was supposed to be apprehending the Count?"

"Busy with other things, I suppose. He doesn't work for me, you know."

"Ah."

We sat in uncomfortable quiet, staring into our mugs and sipping our beer.

"What did we learn at the castle?" Holmes continued. "But for the Barings plot, almost *nil*. While we were gone, however, Lord Anstruther committed suicide rather than have the truth about his Italian mistress become public, a shipment of gold bullion intended for the Bank of England disappeared in transit, and my brother Mycroft was summoned to the Palace. I have no doubt that the latter events are tied into the Argentine situation, all while we were off chasing wild geese. I must continue."

"Holmes, please, drop this for my sake."

"Do you insist, Watson?"

"I do, Holmes. I must. I have my Mary back again. Please give everything you have to Gregson."

Holmes sighed. "Your wish is my command," he said grudgingly.

CHAPTER SEVEN: VAN HELSING

Dr. Watson's Journal

September 25, 1890

New game is afoot!

Despite recent travails, I have decided to return to Baker Street for a few days.

Holmes and I have been avoiding one another since our encounter with the evil Count Dracula. I told Holmes that it was best if I devote my full attention to Mary's recovery, but the truth is that his willingness, even eagerness to risk her life for the sake of this case nettled me deeply, and until recently I have been unable to abide his company.

Nor has Holmes sought mine; though he would never admit it, he is ashamed of his behavior and is too proud to apologise. Left to him, our friendship, our partnership, might have ended. Yet no matter how upset I am with him, I cannot bear to lose my closest and dearest friend. We have had too many adventures together to part for long.

Mary is recuperating beautifully. The colour is back in her cheeks, and she has come back to herself. As with Holmes, Mary's sharp canines have fallen out, to be replaced with white, even teeth. Her neck wounds have been slow to heal, but her spirits have come back, and I think it is safe to leave her alone again. So far, the Count has kept his word, but garlic hangs in our every window.

There is more to my visit than missing Holmes' companionship. Both Gregson and Lestrade have called on me, saying that Holmes has not been himself since we returned to London. When Sherlock Holmes shows signs of melancholy and *ennui*, I worry. He has the finest mind and keenest intellect I have ever been privileged to encounter, but the price he pays for it can be terribly dear.

Naturally, not much progress has been made in locating Dracula; Lestrade believes he has returned to Transylvania. I hope it's true.

Thanks to a letter from Mrs. Mina Harker, we now know that Jonathan somehow survived Castle Dracula and was in the care of nuns in Buda-Pesth while we were looking for him. Mina joined him there, and they married. No doubt we were within a few miles of the happy couple as our train chugged its way back toward London. Our trip and travail had been for nothing.

"There is no way you could have known, Holmes," I said gently, pouring coffee in the Baker Street sitting room. "All Harker's belongings were there, and if fifty boxes of earth were being shipped out, it's perfectly natural to assume that a body was hidden in one of them."

"So once again we learn the value of keeping our mouths shut until we have all the facts," Holmes said with a sigh. "I can only hope our friend Dr. Doyle talks you out of publishing this fiasco."

I never will. There is no pleasure in chronicling failure. Holmes is not always successful, and I have even seen him completely stymied once or twice. But I see no reason to put those tales before my readers; they want to thrill to the triumph of his exceptional intellect, as do I.

"Not to worry, my dear fellow," I replied. "No one would believe it anyway."

We fell into a long, comfortable silence that is only possible between longtime friends. It was my quiet, fervent hope that Holmes would be consulted in the disappearance of Silver Blaze, favoured to win the Wessex Cup next week. Indeed, my only wonder is that he has not already been mixed up in this extraordinary case, which is the one topic of conversation through the length and breadth of England. The horse has vanished, and its trainer, John Straker, has been murdered.

Yet he has said not one word about it. My companion rambled about the room with his chin upon his chest and his brows knitted, charging and recharging his pipe with the strongest black tobacco, and absolutely deaf to any of my questions or remarks.

Work was just what he needed, and it was with relief that I heard him say at last, "I am afraid, Watson, that I shall have to go," as we sat down together to our breakfast this morning.

"Go! Where to?"

"To Dartmoor; to King's Pyland."

By this point, fresh editions of every paper had been sent up by our news agent, only to be glanced over and tossed down into a corner, so I was not surprised when he finally said it.

"I should be most happy to go down with you if I should not be in the way," said I, perhaps with a bit too much hope in my voice.

"My dear Watson, you would confer a great favour upon me by coming. And I think that your time will not be misspent, for there are points about the case which promise to make it an absolutely unique one. We have, I think, just time to catch our train at Paddington, and I will go further into the matter upon our journey. You would oblige me by bringing with you your very excellent field-glass."

And so it happened that an hour or so later I found myself in the corner of a first-class carriage flying along en route for Exeter, while Sherlock Holmes, with his sharp, eager face framed in his ear-flapped travelling-cap, dipped rapidly into the bundle of fresh papers which he had procured at Paddington. We had left Reading far behind us before he thrust the last one of them under the seat and offered me his cigar-case.

I lay back against the cushions, puffing at my cigar, while Holmes, leaning forward, with his long, thin forefinger checking off the points upon the palm of his left hand, gave me a sketch of the events which had led to our journey. I took copious notes, happy to be back at the chase again, but one more thing needed to be done. The Harkers now live in Exeter, and if we alighted there and caught the next train to Tavistock, we had a two-hour window to call on them and, with any luck, close this part of the Dracula case. If this were not done, it might niggle at Holmes for months.

"Quite right, Watson," he replied cheerfully when I made the suggestion. "Better sooner than later. We owe them our congratulations, and there are a few minor points I should like to clear up. It will also be an opportunity to gain fresh news of the Count, who seems to have vanished. At least, he has not visited his estate in London for a while. Two hours ought to be enough."

To my surprise, the cab took us up a long cobblestone drive to a sizeable estate on the outskirts of Exeter. The two-story brick house dated back to Georgian times.

Gardeners worked busily trimming tall green hedges, and several workmen preceded us up the white marble steps to the door.

"I thought Harker was a penurious junior solicitor," I said.

"Last week, he was," Holmes replied. "You ought to keep an eye on the death notices, Watson. Peter Hawkins died suddenly. This was his home; I gather he left it to the Harkers. Perhaps he knew he had not long to live."

"Aren't you the least bit suspicious?"

"Very. They've moved in a little quickly, don't you think?"

I pounded the ornate brass doorknocker, and a pale young girl with wide, dark eyes and brunette hair pinned closely to her skull, answered.

"Dr. Van Helsing?" she asked, looking at me.

"What?" I ejaculated. "Abraham Van Helsing?"

Holmes presented his card. "I am Sherlock Holmes, and this is my colleague, Dr. Watson. Is Mrs. Harker at home?"

The girl stared at me. "So many doctors," she said, and closed the door.

Mina Harker presently greeted us, and though her hair was bound in a prim bun and she wore mourning, rarely have I seen such sunshine from a smile. She embraced Holmes warmly, to his distinct discomfort, and when I held her briefly, I felt a rapid heartbeat. I wondered if a fresh difficulty with her husband had arisen.

Inside was a foyer with a wide staircase to the right. A stained-glass window illuminated the hallway with soft, warm colours suggesting the autumn that was to come, and it was obvious that changes were being made. Light squares on the creamy white walls indicated that pictures had been removed. A large country landscape dominated the left wall.

Under it was a table piled with unanswered correspondence, small boxes, and a few workman's tools, while larger boxes were stacked along the walls. The thick oak double doors on the left were open, revealing the parlor, also somewhat disarrayed, and it was in there Mina Harker led us.

"Mary, please bring tea," she said. "Mr. Holmes, Dr. Watson, the sight of you is the best news I've had since we came home! What brings you here?"

"We are on our way to King's Pyland," said Holmes, "and this seemed as good an opportunity as any to congratulate you and your resourceful husband."

Mina handed me a cup.

"If only he was here," she replied. "I know he's dyi— eager to meet you. Unfortunately, this best of circumstances has come at the worst of times."

"Mr. Hawkins was close to you."

Mina nodded. "I mourn Lucy Westenra as well. She was my closest friend, and was to have been married Sunday, but she took ill and died just two days after Mr. Hawkins."

We offered our condolences, but Holmes' eyes narrowed like a hawk's at this news.

Tears filled Mina Harker's eyes as she continued, "Mr. Holmes, I feel as though a house has fallen on me," she said. "First, Mr. Hawkins invited us here to spend the night. He told us that he was leaving everything to Jonathan because he had no living relations and that Jonathan had been as a son to him, and not twelve hours later he was dead!"

"What?" Holmes ejaculated.

"And poor Arthur's father died the next day, and my dearest Lucy the day after that! Mr. Holmes, everyone whose life touches mine dies! I am the angel of death!"

I assumed that Holmes knew who this Arthur was, but he gave me no sign.

Mina wept freely and now Holmes, who so nearly recoiled from her embrace a few minutes ago, placed her head on his shoulder. The wolf bite hadn't fully healed and he winced, but he let that good lady sob gently until she regained herself. I poured brandy from a decanter on the sideboard.

"I am sorry," she said, accepting the glass. "Please understand, so much has happened so fast."

"Of course, Mrs. Harker," said Holmes. "That you can still run a household and help your husband with so many of his new responsibilities is admirable, and I expect that you are the one looked to by many in times of crisis such as this."

"It is true," she said, "but without Lucy I have no one to tell it to."

"Who is Arthur?" I asked.

"Arthur Holmwood, now Lord Godalming."

I saw Holmes file this nugget away. "He was to marry Miss Westenra."

"Yes."

"How did she die?"

"She suffered some sort of animal bite and lost a lot of blood." Holmes and I exchanged a glance. "Dr. Seward thinks she contracted a disease from it."

"Dr. Seward?" I asked.

"John Seward, he runs an asylum in London. He was close to Lucy. One of her suitors once, as a matter of fact."

"What was his diagnosis?" I continued as Holmes, his gaze alert, sat back and steepled his fingers.

"It didn't seem to be a disease he understood. That's why he called in Dr. Van Helsing."

Though I did my best not to show it, I did not regard this as good news. I have been doing much reading on vampirism, and comparing the legends to modern medical research, in case there is something more to my wife's recent illness than the rantings of a deranged Transylvanian nobleman. Van Helsing's name figures prominently in the literature. He is not highly regarded in most of the medical community. He has written several articles trying to cite science to support superstitions of the sort we encountered in Transylvania; he even accepts lycanthropy. He has developed radical treatments for some illnesses, and it is rumoured that he experiments on his patients.

As far as either Holmes or I can tell, Dracula is doing it all from stagecraft. There isn't anything he does that can't be faked by a skilled stage magician. Certainly when there is thick fog and five trained wolves to hold your attention, you aren't likely to notice the sleight of hand. The only thing I can't account for is the sharpening of his victims' teeth; it is unknown to medical science at this time. Perhaps I can persuade Holmes to add that phenomenon to his rambling list of scientific researches.

"What did Van Helsing do to her?" I wanted to know.

"I don't know. I was on the Continent for most of this, and neither Dr. Seward nor Dr. Van Helsing will tell me anything. They seem to think I am too delicate."

"Most women do not have your determination or

common sense," Holmes said. "I see you have been typing something other than your husband's correspondence."

Mina blushed.

"Yes," she said, "there's something else. Jonathan kept a journal of his adventures in shorthand, and I have been transcribing it."

Holmes' eyes brightened. "Is it here? It might answer many questions."

Mina nodded. "I'll get it for you."

She returned with a thick manuscript. Holmes ignored the first third, I assume going directly to the entries dealing with Harker's time at Castle Dracula.

I touched Mina's arm and cocked my head toward the door.

"If you'll excuse us, Mr. Holmes," she said, "I should like to give Dr. Watson a brief tour of the grounds."

"Don't take too long, Watson," he replied. "We'll need to leave here in half an hour if we expect to catch our train."

"How did Mr. Hawkins die?" I asked once we stepped into the sunshine.

"Dr. Watson! Are you a detective, too?"

"Not if you believe Holmes. No, it just seems odd that he would make you and Jonathan the sole beneficiaries of his estate and then die immediately."

She smiled. "Oh, no. He was elderly and afflicted with gout. He had not long to live, though of course we all wish he were still with us."

We had strolled to a bench by a small pond. On seeing us, a pair of brown ducks left the water and approached, evidently expecting a snack.

"Poor things," Mina said. "Mr. Hawkins liked to give them stale bread."

The ducks glared at us briefly, then returned to their pond.

"You said you'd been invited to stay the night?" I asked.

"Yes. Mr. Hawkins felt terrible guilt for what had happened to Jonathan. Surely he could not have known Count Dracula's plans when he sent Jonathan to Roumania."

I suppressed my first thought and said, "No, of course not." We walked in silence for a moment, and then I asked, "Was there an inquest?"

She shook her head. "The coroner saw no need to conduct one. He said the cause of death was obvious."

"Who found him?"

"Mary, our serving-girl, at eight the next morning." Mina checked her watch. "I have to get back," she said. "Another guest is coming, and your train won't wait."

We saw Holmes in the hallway as we returned; he was putting out a cigarette in an ashtray on the foyer table.

"I took the liberty of a quick look round, Mrs. Harker," said he. "I hope you don't mind. Thank you for a glimpse at that most illuminating journal. If you can find the time, I would greatly appreciate a copy for my own files, and of course I am eager to compare our experiences with those of your husband. You must let us know when your lives become less eventful."

We said our good-byes and she stepped inside, even as her next guest's coach approached. Curious, we lingered as he alighted.

Out stepped a man in his sixties, carrying a Gladstone

bag. His broad chest and burly build clearly indicated peasant stock, though his head was rather larger than it should have been. His square jaw and bushy eyebrows also indicated ancestry from the farms. He wore his graying reddish hair rather long for a medical man, and his penetrating blue gaze, his eyes tinged with red, denoted intelligence and resolve.

Holmes stepped forward and extended his hand.

"It is an honour to meet you, Dr. Van Helsing."

The man seemed taken aback.

"Permit me to introduce my colleague, Dr. John Watson," he continued. "I am Sherlock Holmes."

Relief splashed across Van Helsing's face.

"*Ach*, of course Madam Mina would summon you!" he exclaimed in a heavy Dutch accent. "I am indeed Abraham Van Helsing. Fool that I am, I should have consulted you sooner."

"For what?" I asked.

"Has she not told you? About Miss Lucy?"

"Precious little, I'm afraid," Holmes replied.

"I am not surprised. Absent was Miss Mina for much of what happened."

"What did happen?"

"There, we must separate what we know to be true from what the authorities will accept. Miss Lucy was my patient, and what I have told the coroner is that she died from loss of blood due to internal haemorrhage."

"Caused by?" I asked.

"How so to put this? Miss Lucy's blood was taken from her. She had been bitten by a creature, that is certain. The marks have others seen. But where is the blood?"

"You found none?"

Van Helsing said nothing.

"Perhaps excreted through stool?" I continued, though I knew the answer.

"Nothing so commonplace. We gave her many transfusions, but it was not enough."

"Transfusions!" I was aghast. "Doctor, surely you know that transfusions are risky and unreliable, and only used as a last resort. We don't yet know why some succeed and others fail. How many did you give her?"

"Four."

"My God! From whom?"

Van Helsing's gaze went from my shocked face to Holmes' inscrutable one, and he said, "I see that I was mistaken." He scribbled a note on the back of a calling card, and handed it to Holmes. "I am staying at the Berkeley," he said. "I would like to talk further, but perhaps now is not the time for business to discuss." Then he knocked on the door with great ceremony.

"Don't you know the danger you put her in?" I shouted at Van Helsing's back. "Most transfusions don't work! If you signed the death certificate, I shall demand inquiries!"

Holmes tugged at my arm.

"We have a train to catch," he said.

Holmes had little to say until we were back on the train. Just as well; I was ruminating upon what to do about Van Helsing's startling admission.

In many ways, the medical profession is like a secret society. Each member watches out for the others, and woe betide the doctor who exposes the perfidies of another. To do so is to lose the trust of one's colleagues; we have all had to handle extraordinary and difficult cases and have had to make snap judgments in an emergency. Naturally, we make mistakes. What outsider can pass judgment on that?

But sometimes this professional incest goes too far. It is one thing to look with sympathy on another whose problems you share, and quite another to turn a blind eye to evil or incompetence.

Holmes has often said that a doctor gone wrong is the worst of villains, for he has nerve and he has knowledge. To that I might add perfect positioning to dispose of the evidence. While I have never done so, it is common practice for doctors to conceal minor mistakes in order to protect themselves against litigation.

So the practices of men like Van Helsing tend to grow, like tumors, across the larger medical community. They persuade the families they have done everything possible when in fact it is they who have dug the victim's grave. I wonder if we have enough to go to the police.

"A pretty problem in Exeter," said Holmes. "What do you know of Van Helsing?"

"I know now that he is a dangerous quack!" I exclaimed. "You must be aware of his reputation, Holmes; he tries to marry science and superstition. I can't deny that he has had his share of successes, but I am sure it is only these that keep him in the medical profession."

"I'm afraid I don't know as much as I should about transfusions," Holmes admitted.

"The science of blood is still a mystery," said I. "Your reagent, Holmes, is one of the strongest advances we've had in understanding it in years. You have proven that blood can be identified through chemical reaction, which in turn tells us what some of those chemicals are. We know that sometimes, blood from one man can safely flow in the veins of another, but most of the time it simply doesn't work. In Afghanistan, I saw the blood of a Hindoo used to save the life of one of our officers, but I took that to be a miracle. Most of the time, transfusion patients get worse, or die. Like Lucy Westenra."

"Perhaps that has something to do with Van Helsing's vigil at her grave last night," Holmes said.

"Really, Holmes!"

"My dear Watson, you saw the same things I did. Didn't you see his eyes?"

"Blue."

"And red."

"Meaning he hasn't slept well."

"Not recently. Correct. Anything else?"

"I wasn't looking closely," I said. "I couldn't believe what I was hearing from the man. I was thinking about that."

"So you did not see the crucifix concealed under his shirt."

"No."

"Nor the Hampstead Heath clay on his boots."

"No."

"Nor the lily petal stuck to his right heel."

"All I notice is that my cigar has gone out," I mumbled with exasperation. "How do you know he was at Lucy Westenra's grave?"

I relit my cigar, and a fresh cigarette for Holmes.

"Where else would he have been? She was his only patient in England. Your assumption that I know something of Van Helsing's reputation is correct, Watson. But I don't know which way to take it."

"What do you mean?"

"Van Helsing may be sincere, and is waiting for Miss Westenra to rise from the dead so that he can apply a superstitious remedy to put her down. Or, he may realize exactly what he has done with the transfusions, and may be using vampire superstition to cover up his own incompetence in the matter. If he can get others to believe she is a vampire, and she is disposed of as if she were, there would be no way to prove the transfusions were responsible for her death."

"That's monstrous, Holmes!"

"That may be, but it will have to wait. Right now, millions of bettors need us to find a missing horse."

Not least myself, I thought. My wound pension is so tiny that it barely qualifies as pocket money, so I usually take it to the track. Pity I have never been able to entice Holmes to join me.

CHAPTER EIGHT: SHERLOCK HOLMES PAYS A CALL

Jonathan Harker's Journal

September 29, 1890

A momentous occasion: to-day I was called upon by none other than the great Mr. Sherlock Holmes! I should have expected his visit; he was in the house the other day, on his way to Devonshire at the behest of Colonel Ross, whose great racehorse Silver Blaze has disappeared.

In Mr. Holmes I thought I had an important ally, for Count Dracula saw me on the streets of London last week, and I have lost a great deal of sleep wondering when and how his revenge will come. That he has something planned I do not doubt, for no more diabolical mind walks the earth.

But I cannot get anyone to listen to me. When I went to Scotland Yard, I was referred to an Inspector Tobias Gregson, who told me that not only was the Count not wanted for any crimes in Transylvania, but that we in England should be pleased that he has chosen to favour our fair clime with his presence! Without evidence of a crime, Gregson told me, there is little the police can do.

It is absurd to expect the modern educated Englishman to accept a story like mine at face value, but Sherlock Holmes was in the castle, and had to have seen what I had seen. Yet not only does he disbelieve my story, he has shaken my self-confidence to the core. I hardly know whether to trust my senses now.

But Dr. Van Helsing, whose mind surely is as great as that of Mr. Holmes, believes my story in every detail. Holmes is wrong. He must be wrong!

I was alone in the office Sunday afternoon when I heard three sharp knocks on the door. I was surprised; I had told no one but Mina I was coming in. I have been trying to get my mind off Count Dracula, and Mr. Hawkins left such a mound of work that it's the perfect thing.

(*Mem.*, must meet Prof. Moriarty soon and familiarize myself with his correspondence. A good third of the workload seems to be coming from him, and he appears to have had a hand in shipping the Count's boxes to England. No correspondence since Sept. 13.)

The door opened to reveal one of the tallest, leanest men I've ever seen, narrow of face and with a mesmerizing gaze that seemed to reach back into my mind and read everything there. His dark frock coat and his dark hair, thin and swept back, together with his beak-like nose and pale skin gave me a start. I have been thinking too much of vampires lately, a feeling that did not fade when he ran a cold, critical gaze over me.

Then his features softened somewhat and he presented his card.

"It is a pleasure to meet you at last, Mr. Jonathan Harker," he said. "I am Sherlock Holmes."

Relief! Mina has told me much of his exertions in my behalf.

"At last!" I cried. "My wife cannot sing your praises highly enough."

"I am pleased to hear that, though she is hardly justified in doing so."

"You gave her the hope she so desperately needed while her childhood friend was wasting away. Losing us both would have left her in despair, and she might well be dead of a broken heart by now. It was by God's mercy alone that I escaped and survived."

"I perceive that to be true," he said, "though I see you found some other means of egress from the castle other than crawling down the wall. The catacombs, perhaps?"

"The powder magazine," I said. "There are hand-holds carved into the exterior walls in various parts of the castle, and the one I used led to an old storage room. I found muskets and gunpowder casks there."

"That would be the western face of the castle."

"Yes."

I led him to the office and offered him a cigarette, which he accepted.

"I found a tunnel in there," I continued, "and it connected to a cave that came out in a copse by the road, about a quarter-mile from the castle. I imagine it was intended for the purpose of ambushing marauders. I was starved, feverish, and delirious. I have few clear recollections before my rescue in Buda-Pesth."

"I should like to hear your recollections, if you please."

"Haven't you read my journal?"

"Yes, but I have not read all of it. Perhaps you have new insights since then."

"Not the least that Count Dracula has established himself in London. I saw him with my very eyes not a week ago."

Holmes' eyes widened with interest. "Are you sure it was he?"

"There is no doubt, but somehow the Count has

taken fifty years off his appearance! The Dracula I knew
was an old man; he could have been between seventy and
eighty. The man I saw in Hyde Park looked my age, but I
can never forget those ghastly red eyes, those feral animal
features, nor those wolf's teeth. It was Dracula, mark my
word."

"I believe you," Holmes said evenly. "Pray give me the
benefit of your experiences."

It took nearly an hour. The tale grew easier in the
telling, and I realized what Holmes was trying to do; fresh-
en my recollection so he could ask pertinent questions.
When I finished, he asked, "Do you believe those women
were vampires?"

"With my heart and soul," I replied.

"Did they take your blood?"

"They would have, had not the Count stopped them."

"Was that to be your fate? To be given to them when
Dracula had no further need of you?"

"Of course."

"If they did not take your blood, how did you know
they were vampires?"

"I saw them materialize out of the moonlight, Mr.
Holmes. No earthly creatures can do that."

"They can with mirrors. I have exposed several fake
mediums, and know their methods."

"There are no mirrors at Castle Dracula. Surely you
know why."

"Yes, but I am not sure you do."

"I know you are a man of science," I said, "but I cannot deny my experiences. Every word I wrote is as true as
Mina's heart."

"That you fully believe it I have no doubt," said

Sherlock Holmes. "But I was attacked by those women, too. They drank my blood, and made me drink theirs."

"My God!"

"And yet I sit before you, in the pink of health."

Begging his pardon, I rose and went to the washroom, where I keep a spare shaving-kit. Retrieving a glass, I returned to my office. Holmes' face was clearly visible in it.

"You could have spotted my reflection in the windows," he said. "But as you see, I am no vampire."

"How did you escape that horrid fate?"

"I, too, fell ill with fever and delirium, but my partner Dr. Watson pulled me through." He leaned forward in his chair. "Please understand, Mr. Harker, that I do not doubt your veracity. I simply find vampirism itself difficult to accept. I believe Count Dracula does everything he can to promote the illusion of a vampire colony at his castle to maintain his power in the province. Fear is an excellent means of control, especially in a land as riddled in superstition and folklore as is Transylvania."

"Yet you were fooled too, at least for a time."

He took a fresh cigarette from his coat pocket, lit it, and looked at me. Then he smiled, displaying a set of sharp fangs!

I jumped. My hand stole toward the crucifix I now wear at all times, when he opened his mouth and the fangs fell into his hand.*

"Hollow them out and fill the tiny chambers with

---

* Watson does not explain why Holmes did this despite having grown vampire teeth himself. I speculate that Holmes wanted to read Harker's reaction and test his sanity. I also believe that Holmes needed to concoct a rational explanation to mollify the many who would simply refuse to believe in vampires. —SS

extract of belladonna," he said, tossing the false teeth on my desk. Small, clear drops oozed onto my blotter.

"Not enough to kill," Holmes continued, "but enough to induce hallucinations and dizziness once injected into the bloodstream. Practitioners of witchcraft have used it to give themselves visions for centuries. After that, it's just a matter of repeating injections until the victim succumbs, either from the poison or from blood loss, assuming our 'vampire' is really taking any."

"Where did you get those?" I asked.

"I commissioned them from a theatrical supply company."

"That's what you think happened to me?"

"It is a theory that fits the facts. In your case, Dracula poisoned your food to keep you weak, pliant and confused. In my attack, the women used devices similar to these. You were the victim of an elaborate hoax, Mr. Harker, as was I.

"Count Dracula is a madman, but a madman who knows his game to perfection. You will find, I think, that you have yet to directly witness any miracles or magic. Between misdirection or terror, someone as skilled and experienced as Count Dracula can make almost anyone believe almost anything."

"Why do all that if he were going to kill me anyway?"

"People can escape from Castle Dracula, Mr. Harker, as you yourself have proved. Yet, even now you are unwilling to believe the probable over the impossible. To a mind as insidious as the Count's, the illusion must be maintained at all times."

"Did you know this when the women attacked you?"

Holmes shook his head. "I was sick for days. Only

recently have I been able to construct a hypothesis and test it. Poison, stagecraft and terror, Mr. Harker. There are no vampires."

The confidence imbued in me by Van Helsing sank like a stone. Doubts about the whole adventure crept back into my soul.

"It sounds so obvious when you explain it that way," I replied.

"Surely it is less frightening than worrying about vampires," he said.

"How did the Count make himself so much younger?" I asked.

"How close were you when you saw him?"

"I spotted him across the street, in Hyde Park."

"If you were closer, I expect you would have spotted a wig and makeup." Holmes stubbed his cigarette out and then asked, "I encountered him myself a few weeks ago, and I would place his age at about five-and-thirty."

"Did you see any makeup?"

"No, it was too dark. But then, he might have made himself up to be old when he met you. A few strokes with a comb and some talcum powder can add years. Perhaps he is a younger man who, for reasons of his own, wished to appear old to you."

I looked at the fake fangs on my blotter and realized it could all be true. I began to distrust my own memories.

"Mr. Harker, we were both attacked. You did not die, though you were intended to, and I did not die. The fact that we have both fully recovered and can shave without fear ought to tell you something, don't you think?"

I could think of nothing to say.

"May I ask about something else?" he inquired. "What

were Mr. Hawkins' dealings with Professor James Moriarty? Mr. Hawkins was Moriarty's solicitor."

"He was, but I haven't met the man yet. I know most of the firm's clients, but Professor Moriarty never came to this office as far as I know. Why?"

"Because evil, like water, finds its own level. Are you aware that none of Count Dracula's boxes of earth was ever examined by Customs?"

"I'm still straightening out the correspondence, Mr. Holmes."

"Of course. May I ask how Mr. Hawkins died?"

I paused, wondering why he wanted to know such things.

"Not that it has anything to do with Transylvania," said I, "but between old age and gout his time was coming, and he knew it."

"Is that why he invited you and Mrs. Harker to dinner the night he died?"

"I believe so. I have no reason not to."

"You were the only guests?"

"Yes."

"And the servant girl?"

"She has been in the house for a little over three months. I understand that her mother is dead and that her father is in Dartmoor, but for what she won't tell us. Why are you asking me these things?"

"Everything may be relevant, Mr. Harker. What is the girl's last name?"

"Brooks."

"May I take a look at Professor Moriarty's correspondence?"

Now I took umbrage. "With all due respect, Mr.

Holmes, you ask too much! A client's confidentiality is sacred!"

"As no one knows better than myself," he replied with a small chuckle. "You just passed a character test, Mr. Harker, and I am pleased to say that Mrs. Harker has chosen very well. As I expect you know, I have pressing business in Devonshire. But once your lives settle down, I would be honoured to have you and your sterling wife join me for dinner in Baker Street."

He rose to go. I'm sure my relief was obvious; Sherlock Holmes can be an intimidating man, and I should hate to have him stand against me.

September 30, 1890

I do not know for sure, but I am nearly certain that someone has been in my offices since yesterday.

Everything is where it should be, but small things tell. Stacks of letters are just a little bit further to the right than they ought to be, and a letter from Professor Moriarty opened to my merest touch. His letters usually need to be slit with a letter opener. I suspect an agent of Count Dracula has been here, trying to divine my plans.

Whether Mr. Holmes believes in vampires or not, I am certain they walk the earth, and I know they do not need doors to enter buildings! All the doors and windows are locked, as I left them; who else could have come in here?

There is no time to worry about this now. Far more urgent is finding out what happened to all those boxes of unholy earth the Count has brought into my country. I must hear what Mr. Billington has to say. Off to Whitby!

CHAPTER NINE:
LUCY WESTENRA'S CRYPT

Dr. Watson's Journal

October 1, 1890

Back in London again, following another triumph for Sherlock Holmes in the recovery of Silver Blaze. We have even earned the forgiveness of Colonel Ross, who paid the price for publicly doubting Holmes. Not only that, I made a tidy packet on the race, which means a gift for Mary. I have become a contortionist in my efforts to make her happy and speed her recovery.

"I imagine you're looking forward to the evening editions," I said to Holmes after Colonel Ross left Baker Street yesterday afternoon.

"Let Inspector Gregory have his day," he replied. "He has a promising career ahead of him, if he is willing to learn, and it was he who gave us the initial facts. I see no reason to impede him. I much prefer your versions of my cases, my dear Watson, though you make what ought to be simple instructions in logic and science far too romantic."

"Thank you, Holmes," said I. "Now what else have you been up to? I came here to enjoy your company, and I've hardly seen you these past few days."

"I have been watching Jonathan Harker being drawn into a maelstrom," he replied.

"Holmes, you promised to drop this. What of Mary?"

"Your house is redolent with garlic and crucifixes.

That avenue is closed to Dracula, Watson. We may now try again."

With a sigh, I took out my notebook, and made a note to contact Gregson immediately.

"Harker spotted the Count in Hyde Park just over a week ago, looking much as we saw him. His skill with makeup must rival my own." He paused and continued, "It so happens, Watson, that Peter Hawkins personally arranged the *Demeter's* passage, and did so at the behest of Professor Moriarty. I saw the correspondence myself in what is now Harker's office."

"I'm surprised he let you read it."

Holmes smiled with a touch of mischief in his eyes.

"As I am sure Harker would be," he said. "There is no doubt in my mind that this man made it possible for Count Dracula to get into England at Moriarty's behest. I am also certain that Peter Hawkins did not die a natural death. But he truly did love Jonathan Harker, Watson, and did not know the nature of the bargain struck between Moriarty and Dracula. I believe that Hawkins discovered Harker's intended fate, objected to it, and planned to go to the police.

"Hawkins knew he was doomed for this, and he acted hastily to ensure his estate would fall into trusted hands. Just in time, for the night he announced his bequest, an escaped convict by the name of Kraven Brooks was let into the kitchen and hidden in the root cellar."

"Wait a second, Holmes. Who is Kraven Brooks?"

"He is the father of Mary Brooks, the Harkers' servant girl. Once I discovered that, much became clear. My encounter with him happened a year or so before you and I met. Brooks' Christian name proved prophetic—'craven' exactly describes the manner in which he has conducted his life. He is a thief, blackmailer and real estate swindler whose oversized sense of self-importance led him to poison a journalist about to expose one of his schemes. I intervened and the journalist survived, and Brooks was sentenced to thirty years in Dartmoor. But he escaped about six months ago, and it was only natural that he would seek out his daughter."

Holmes lit a cigarette, and continued, "It was Hawkins' custom to have Mary Brooks bring a cup of warm milk before bed to help him sleep. Unbeknownst to Mary, her father poisoned the milk, hastening Hawkins' death. As Hawkins was known to be infirm, no one would question it."

"How do you know all this?"

Holmes opened a drawer and produced a small glass vial.

"I found this in the kitchen while you and Mrs. Harker took your stroll. I haven't identified the poison yet, but I believe it is tropical in origin. Where would Brooks get that, and what reason could he have for poisoning his daughter's employer? The footprints in the root cellar don't match those of anyone who lives there; the stride and shoe size are consistent with Brooks, as I remember. I have given the case to the Exeter constabulary, who are now searching the countryside for him. I expect Mary shall give him up soon enough. Between them, we'll have the truth. But right now, we have more interesting fish to fry."

"Oh?"

"Don't you want a look at the grave Van Helsing has been watching? Meet me for lunch at Jack Straw's Castle, and be sure to wear black. Bring your medical bag."

Evening. If I have anything to say about it, the career of Abraham Van Helsing is about to come to a sudden and overdue end.

What I witnessed this afternoon goes beyond villainy. I can barely steady my pen as I write this, for the man is so far gone in his fantasies that no act, no matter how grotesque or obscene, is beyond his conscience.

Jack Straw's Castle is an inn in Hampstead Heath, located where Spaniards Road meets the North End Way. Not seeing my friend, I requested a table in the back and sipped a glass of beer until an animated Holmes burst in the door, dressed in black and carrying a Gladstone bag similar to my own.

"You may need something stronger than that after you hear what I have to say," said he, signalling for sandwiches. "There have been extraordinary doings in this neighborhood."

"Oh?"

"Surely you have read newspaper accounts of children being abducted by a mysterious 'Bloofer Lady.'"

I nodded.

"Our link to Count Dracula. She evidently picks the children up, nicks them in the throat, and leaves them for discovery the next morning. Two were found near here just last week. The lady in question matches the description of Miss Westenra."

"You mean the late Miss Westenra, Holmes."

"Do I? In any event, one of these children is recuperating from a Bloofer Lady attack at the North London Hospital, under the care of a Dr. Vincent. Do you know him, Watson?"

"I'm afraid not."

"Pity. An earnest man, if not a particularly observant one. He is also one of Van Helsing's disciples; the man seems to have stashed them all over London. Unfortunately, Van Helsing and Seward talked to him before I did, and Vincent is inclined to take the views of his former master."

"What is Dr. Vincent's opinion?"

"The lad had the usual bite marks on the neck, so Vincent thinks that the child was bitten by a bat, possibly of foreign origin, possibly carrying a disease. At least when he used the word 'vampire,' he was referring to the bats found in South America. The lad is recovering nicely, and he'll probably go home in a day or two. He has little memory of his ordeal. He barely remembers Miss Westenra."

"Vincent saw no indication of human bite marks?"

"No, nor did I."

Our sandwiches arrived. Holmes, apparently famished, attacked his with gusto.

"It's only in the last day that I've been able to take this case up again," he said. "Fortunately, Lestrade is having a hard time of it, and asked me to take a hand before another child disappears. So if we get caught, we'll have an explanation."

"An explanation for what?"

"For standing over an empty coffin."

We took a cab to the nearby Child's Hill neighborhood, where we alighted near one of the churches. Holmes walked briskly along the street toward the churchyard gates, which opened inward to a wide avenue lined with yew trees, whose leaves were changing colour and falling as autumn claimed the season. Obelisks, cenotaphs, and mausoleums of all styles and stone gave the place an air of peace, and of history. A warm breeze crossed our brows, rustling the leaves and carrying a slight aroma of fresh earth.

Holmes strode in as though he owned the place. It struck me that perhaps the Holmes family tomb might well be here; he has told me so little of his family history that any new information would be welcome, and I may one day come back on my own.

We slowed down. It was best not to give the mourners at a nearby service the impression that we had come on a mission. Indeed, we passed the Westenra tomb and found a stone bench, out of view.

"Half one," said Holmes, checking his pocket watch. "They should be leaving soon, and then we can get to work."

"What sort of work?"

"I don't think Lucy Westenra ever died," said he. "I believe that she has come under Dracula's spell and was coerced into his horrid harem. Drugging her and allowing her out only at night would be an excellent way to reinforce the delusion that she is a vampire. A day or so of being entombed alive would break many a strong man's spirit, let alone what it would do to a girl bedridden for weeks."

"You've seen her?" said I.

"No, but Miss Westenra is overdue for another attack. I am hoping to find proof in the tomb. I need to take something to Lestrade so that he will have a legal reason to search Count Dracula's estate at Carfax. Independent, unimaginative eyes would be most helpful in a case like this. Ah!"

The funeral was breaking up, and not long after, the

sexton closed and locked the gates. Once we were alone, we made our way to the dark, ancient, and grim tomb of the Westenra family. Holmes fumbled in his bag and produced a large, rusty skeleton key, unlocking the black steel door.

"Note that someone has been here," said he, "and tried to seal this tomb. There are bits of putty in every cranny about the door."

A thick stench hit us when we pushed the door open. That foul air held not only more than two hundred years of dank decay, added to it were the sickly scents of rotting flowers, fresh garlic, decaying corpses, and rancid blood. That last is a repulsive scent I would know anywhere, a stench that brings back to me the horrors of battlefields strewn with the dead and dying, of limbs rank with gangrene, of life dripping away from soldiers and civilians alike. None of my adventures since my return to London has brought back those memories so forcefully as did that foetid cloud from the Westenra death chamber.

Holmes cried out and clamped a handkerchief over his face. When at last that ghastly reek dissipated, we went inside.

"I'll need your most professional manner, Doctor," he said at last, sorrow in his voice. "We are too late."

Holmes fumbled in his bag and found a lantern, which cast a solemn glow inside the sepulchre, casting outsized shadows on the granite walls.

Lucy Westenra's coffin was just inside the door, on a slab to the left. Dozens of footprints were on the floor. The flowers had been piled in a corner, and white wax drippings from candles were evident on the coffin lid.

"Arrogant fool!" Holmes muttered in self-reproach as

he removed a screwdriver from his bag. "One of the reasons I've been so public about the Pennington forgery is to
divert attention from the Bloofer Lady. I thought she'd be
safe! Vanity, thy name is Sherlock Holmes!"

He moved with dervish speed, removing the large
screws that sealed the coffin lid and dropping them on the
floor, chipping away fresh lead solder as he went. Together
we pushed the massive lead shroud off the top and lowered
it quietly to the floor. The sight was horrifying, but before
we could take a close look, a fresh burst of gas sent us outside, where I saw that Holmes was on the edge of shock.

"Watson, what have I done?" he said softly. "Why did
I not act to save her?"

"Perhaps she did die after all," I said. "This is precisely what one ought to expect from opening a coffin."

"She wasn't here Sunday night," he replied. "I came
here at nine o'clock and opened the coffin myself. It was
empty."

"My God, Holmes!"

"I'm sorry I didn't tell you, but I wanted you to see it
with your own eyes. If she wasn't in the coffin, she had to
be alive. Everything else we know about this fits in with
our experiences at the castle. I should have tracked her
down that very night!"

I opened my own bag, and found a flask of brandy.

"For strength, Holmes," I said, handing it to him.

He took a healthy draught, and handed it back to me;
I did the same.

"Perhaps we can help the poor girl yet," said he as he
came back to himself. "We can at least bring her killers to
justice."

Leaving the tomb's door ajar, we examined the scene,

though it took all my experience as a battlefield doctor to keep my nerves steady.

The poor girl had been murdered in the most horrible, gruesome manner. The corpse was drenched in foul blackened blood. A thick wooden stake had been driven with great force through her heart. The villains had cut off the upper portion of the stake, leaving the rest embedded in the corpse. It was sawed in two about an inch above Lucy's breast, with the remainder placed in the coffin along her outer left thigh. I estimate that it must have been close to three feet long, and thick as a baby's arm.

Gruesome enough, but they had gone farther. The girl's head had been cut off with a sharp surgical instrument, and her mouth stuffed with garlic. Yet, even in the face of this desecration, I noticed a look of utter serenity in the poor child's face. Somehow, she had died peacefully.

"How long has she been dead, Doctor?" asked Holmes.

"At first glance, I must say no more than three days."

Holmes saw the empty coffin on Sunday, and now it was Wednesday. My heart sank as I realized that the poor girl probably died on the night Holmes last visited this tomb. All he'd had to do is wait; he just missed her. The painful realization of this truth filled Holmes' eyes and he looked away for a moment.

"I am so sorry," he whispered.

We stopped talking and gazed at the hideous corpse. Holmes, tall, thin and pale in his black garments, with his grim hawkish visage, looked in that moment like a vicar who has irretrievably lost his faith. Rarely have I seen a man so disgusted with himself.

"Only Van Helsing can be responsible," said I after a time. "He has corrupted Seward and God knows who else and murdered a girl in her very grave!"

"I know, Watson," said he. "Would you be so kind as to wait outside while I summon Lestrade?"

October 2, 1890

It is a bitter, dark day for justice.

We took photographs of the poor girl's desecration. Holmes measured every square inch of the tomb and collected several samples. We had Van Helsing in our very palms, and Lestrade dispatched constables to bring him in.

Yet we have been frustrated again. I came round Baker Street for breakfast this morning only to find Holmes in deep, animated conversation with Lestrade and a young man, about thirty, clean-shaven, brown-eyed and wealthy, to judge from the cut of his clothes.

"Lestrade, there is no other way to look at this than as cold-blooded murder!" Holmes was saying as I let myself in. The three men rose to greet me.

"Ah, good morning, Watson," said Holmes, who was clearly holding back an intemperate remark. "Thank God you're here. May I introduce Arthur Holmwood, who recently assumed the title Lord Godalming? He has a mesmerizing tale to tell."

We shook hands; Godalming's grip was firm, strong and callused, like that of a horseman.

"An honour, my lord," said I, and took my usual seat by the fireplace. "What brings you to Baker Street?"

"To be honest, Doctor, I have come here to ask that you and Mr. Holmes cease harassing Dr. Van Helsing and avoid any future involvement in his, or my own, affairs."

"Lord Godalming was affianced to Miss Westenra," Holmes said, "and has inherited her estate."

"I hope you're not implying that I murdered her for her money," Godalming muttered.

"You raised that possibility, not I," said Holmes with irritation. "Doctor, wasn't it your professional opinion that the poor girl had only been dead for three days?"

"The conditions were hardly ideal, Holmes. I gave you my best guess in the circumstances."

"The coffin was empty on Sund—"

"Gentlemen, please!" said Lestrade. "Holmes, you must admit that all we really have is your word for most of this. All we can take to the Crown is evidence of mutilating a corpse."

"For which we had excellent reason," Godalming said bitterly. "Not that I would expect such as yourselves to understand."

Mrs. Hudson brought in tea and Godalming began his tale. Holmes crossed his legs and steepled his fingers in the gesture of concentration I know so well.

"Dr. Van Helsing and Dr. Seward took me and Quincey Morris, my friend from Texas, to Lucy's tomb shortly before midnight Sunday. As I am now its guardian, I had a key, and we went inside.

"I could see at once that the coffin had been opened before, and I was furious with Van Helsing, but he set to work and opened it again. We four looked into it and will all swear that the coffin was empty."

"I know," said Holmes. "Most people do not live in coffins."

Godalming ignored him. "We replaced the lid and locked the tomb. For a while, I dared give myself hope that some horrendous mistake had been made and that the sextons had found her wandering about. How I wanted to believe that! Then Van Helsing did the strangest thing—he crushed some wafers into a wad of putty and wedged it under the door and all around the edges.

"'What are you doing?' Seward asked.

"'I am closing the tomb so that the undead may not enter,' Van Helsing replied.

"'And is that stuff you have put there going to do it?' asked Quincey Morris. 'Great Scott! Is this a game?'

"'It is.'

"I asked Van Helsing what he was using, and he said, 'The Host. I brought it from Amsterdam. I have an Indulgence.'"

"That's—that's sacrilege!" I cried.

"I know, Dr. Watson, but you will soon see why the Professor was right to do it. For as he was completing his grim task, I saw a shimmering figure of white coming toward us down the avenue. Even in the darkness I knew her, but when the clouds parted and the moonlight touched her, there was no doubt; it was my Lucy. She stopped, and I could see she held something close to her breast. She bent her head, and I could see it was a small child, which cried out, either in agony or horror. She came closer to the tomb, clutching it tightly."

Godalming's voice began to thicken with emotion, and tears brimmed in his eyes, but after a moment he continued with his tale.

"At the Professor's signal, we drew back, and when the clouds parted again, my breast was filled with both fascination and revulsion. For though this creature had Lucy's features, and could be no one else, she had changed. Gone was the innocence and purity that I so cherished; this was the face of a cruel, voluptuous harpy."

I shuddered, remembering what similar women had done to the man who now trained his steely, hawklike gaze on Godalming, sparks all but flying from his eyes.

Godalming continued:

"As she advanced, Van Helsing motioned us to form a line between her and the tomb. When she drew close enough, he withdrew the slide from his lantern, and the full force of the illumination brought home the horror of what my Lucy had become. Her teeth, so smooth and white and even, now seemed to have been filed to sharp points, and her breath carried the stench of death. But my heart quailed when I saw what was dripping from her lips and chin. Gentlemen, they were glistening with fresh scarlet blood, blood taken from that unfortunate child!"

Godalming paused, clearly shaken by the memory. I rose to fetch brandy, but Holmes stopped me with a glare.

"Mr. Holmes, Mina Harker has shared what she knows of your adventures in Transylvania. How can you be so sceptical?"

"I take it Mr. Harker has not discussed my visit with him that very morning?"

"No, I haven't seen him," Godalming replied.

"Pray continue with your fascinating narrative."

"I stood as a statue, unable to tear my gaze from this creature who once owned my heart and soul. When she saw us, she hissed like a rattlesnake ready to strike. When she saw me, she flung the child to the ground, as if it were a worn-out rag doll. Recognizing me, she smiled with an evil promise of delights to come, if only I would partake. She opened her arms, beckoning me, and though her evil was a palpable thing, I wanted to fold myself onto her breast and never let her go again."

Holmes nodded, and I could see him struggling with the cloudy memories of his own attack by the harpies at Castle Dracula. So much was clicking into place.

"Quincey tells me that I groaned as she came closer to me.

"'Come to me, Arthur,' said the thing in Lucy's body in the sweetest, most alluring voice. 'Leave these others and come to me. My arms are hungry for you. Come and we can rest together. Come, my husband, come!'

"By now I was in thrall, I confess it. I opened my arms to her, and would have been her slave had not the Professor leaped between us, and waved his little crucifix in her face. She hissed again, and dashed past us to the tomb, where she halted. In frustration, she turned on us, hissed again, and fixed us with a hateful glare.

"'Answer me, my friend,' said Van Helsing to me. 'Am I to proceed with my work?'

"By now I was near collapse, my mind awhirl with horror at what I had almost done. I dropped to my knees and shed tears into my hands.

"'Do as you will, friend; do as you will,' I mumbled. 'There can be no horror like this ever any more!'

"Quincey and Seward grabbed my arms and hauled me to my feet as Van Helsing set to work. He removed some of the putty as Lucy looked on, like a snake at the ready.

"The Professor stepped back, and we all saw it: the woman who carried a child all the way across the graveyard as if it were a toy, the woman who stood before me as real as yourselves, passed through the crack in the tomb door!

"As I stared in disbelief, the Professor replaced the putty. Coming over to me, he said, 'My friend Arthur, you have had sore trial; but after, when you will look back, you will see how it was necessary. You are now in bitter waters, my child. By this time tomorrow, please God, you will have passed them, and have drunk of the sweet waters; so do not mourn overmuch. 'Til then, I shall not ask you to forgive me.'"

I did not know what to think; surely Godalming didn't think we would believe such a story. It's obvious she had a key herself. There are many questions here, but they will go forever unanswered now.

"But that isn't all, is it, Lord Godalming?" prompted Holmes, who now lit a cigarette.

"We went back the following afternoon, and on that day I performed the most horrible, and most compassionate, act of my life. Even though I knew the thing she had become, she was still beautiful to me. At first I trembled when we opened the coffin, but as I gazed down on the wanton expression that fouled her beauty my heart hardened.

"'Is this really Lucy's body, or only a demon in her shape?' I asked Van Helsing.

"'It is her body, and yet not it,' he replied. 'But wait a while, and you shall see her as she was, and is.'

"Then Van Helsing prepared for what was to come. He brought his lantern, of course, a soldering iron and solder, a massive hammer, and a huge wooden stake, about three feet long and sharpened to a fine point.

"My stomach twisted itself at the thought of what he was about to do, and the rational part of my mind screamed at me for believing this was the proper thing.

But I could not deny what I had seen. Van Helsing could see this and he said to me:

"'My friend, if you had kissed her, you would in time, when you had died, have become a vampire yourself. Blessed will be the hand that strikes the blow which sets her free. To this I am willing; but is there none amongst us who has a better right? Will it be no joy to think of hereafter in the silence of the night: 'It was my hand that sent her to the stars; the hand she herself would have chosen?'"

"What could I do under their gaze? The act would be abhorrent in the extreme, but this evil had to end. I was filled with love for Van Helsing, who had sacrificed so much to bring us the truth.

"'My true friend,' I said quietly, 'from the bottom of my broken heart, I thank you. Tell me what I am to do, and I shall not falter!'

"I placed the point of the stake over her heart as Van Helsing began to read the Prayer of the Dead. I trembled for a moment and tried not to look at the face of she whose purity and goodness of heart had been corrupted forever. Even now, I prayed she would open her eyes and tell me this had all been a horrible nightmare. Seward and Quincey began to read, and I summoned all the steel in my soul to bring the hammer down with a single, swift, solid stroke.

"I won't forget that scream to the day I die. It tore through my soul like a bitter, icy wind. But having struck that first blow, I dared not stop. Down came the hammer, again and again, until the tip penetrated the coffin's floor.

"Lucy's sharp white teeth champed together in agony, rending her lips and spreading blood everywhere. She screamed and writhed, her limbs jerking with fierce energy. In a savage frenzy, I kept pounding, and did not stop until her death spasms ceased.

"The hammer fell from my exhausted fingers onto the floor, and I fell back, caught by Quincey and Seward. They eased me onto the floor so I could catch my breath. The others spent a moment in silence looking down on her; at last I joined them.

"What I saw gladdened my heart, and I knew I had done the right thing. For the voluptuous evil that defined her features before had departed. The Lucy that I loved and buried once before lay now in peaceful serenity. I had freed her from the depths of hell.

"I could take no more. I left the others to their gruesome work and never looked back."

We sat in silence to give the poor, tear-eyed man a chance to collect himself; there was no doubt in my mind that he believed it all, but Holmes' expression was dour.

"Lestrade, this is a confession!" he snapped.

"If you'll excuse us, my lord," the inspector said. Godalming waited in the foyer. "The man may not be in his right mind, Holmes, but he is well placed. There simply is no way to prove that Miss Westenra was alive when he mutilated her body. He'll have three witnesses who will swear she was not, and dozens of people saw her in a casket at her funeral."

"It would not be the first time someone was accidentally buried alive."

"There is a signed death certificate," Lestrade continued. "When I went to the North London Hospital and showed Miss Westenra's likeness to the victim there, he didn't remember her. No one has seen her since she died. There is no way to independently verify or disprove his lordship's story. It flies in the face of all logic and all the facts. We just can't prove murder, Holmes. I am satisfied we won't be seeing any more bloofer ladies, and the matter stops there. I can't base an arrest on evidence like this. I'd be laughed out of court."

"Not for the first time, either," Holmes grumbled.

Stepping in, I said, "The body I saw had only been dead for a few days, not several weeks. That must mean something."

"Did you examine it closely?" asked Lestrade. "Was there enough light? In any event, you two had no right to be there."

"Watson, I don't suppose there is any way to investigate the transfusions?"

"No, Holmes, not with a cadaver in that condition. We'll never know the true cause of death."

Holmes sighed with frustration. "Very well, Lestrade. If you won't take this further, I suppose there is no way I can make you."

Godalming returned to the sitting room.

"I prefer not to use my position, Mr. Holmes," Godalming he said, "but I will if it becomes necessary."

"Your heart is at peace?" Holmes asked him. "You are certain you have done the Christian thing?"

My heart filled with loathing for Godalming. How can decapitating the woman one loves be the Christian thing? He admitted Lucy screamed and bled, and Lestrade is letting it go due to his position in society. I doubt the good inspector would hesitate to haul me in if I made such statements. There are times I damn the nobility.

"There is no doubt at all. I am easy in my mind," Godalming said resolutely.

"Then, I suppose, so must we be," Holmes said, defeated. "Good morning, gentlemen."

I offered Holmes a cigar after they left.

"What now?"

Holmes handed me a telegram. "Godalming has already pulled some strings. This came from Mycroft last night."

"My dear Sherlock," the telegram read, "Drop bloofer lady. Nothing to be gained. Home Office furious. I will conduct any further inquiries if necessary. M."

"That poor girl was no more a vampire than you are," Holmes said. "Thanks to my bungling, it's too late. Perhaps I should pack it in and take up beekeeping."

"Nonsense, Holmes," I replied. "Peter Hawkins' murderer can still be brought to justice."

"He was," Holmes replied. "He was found hanging in his cell this morning. Craven, indeed. Ah, well! There are still experiments to be made. Chemicals, at least, are usually predictable."

PART THREE

THE GREAT HIATUS

CHAPTER TEN: THE NAPOLEON
OF CRIME

[Editor's note: Sherlockian scholars have been vexed by the Great Hiatus for more than 100 years. Watson's daily journal sheds new light on the events that led to it, not the least what really happened after the struggle with Professor Moriarty. For reasons that will become obvious, Watson obscured and altered much in "The Final Problem."]

Dr. Watson's Journal

April 27, 1891

The game's afoot, Holmes likes to say, but this time it is we who are the quarry.

I know I ought to be more worried about the state of things than I am, but the truth is I would much rather face Professor Moriarty and his minions than I would my wife right now. Mary seemed to have come back to herself after Holmes and I rescued her from Count Dracula, and for several months we were a normal husband and wife again; we had even resumed our attempts to begin a family.

But during this time her memory concerning the vile Count had fallen into a deep, black hole. She remembered very little of him after that final evening, though small reminders lingered for months; she found it hard to attend church, could not catch a proper night's rest until we finally took the garlic cloves down from our bedroom windows, and stayed either indoors or in the shadows on bright autumn days. But when we took a brief Continental holiday in November, all seemed well.

About two weeks ago, Mary started remembering little bits and pieces of that night, usually in her dreams—hours spent in the woods of Winchester, delirious and cold, clad only in a gossamer nightgown; nasty bursts of nightmare about being menaced by wolves; Dracula's long, sharp teeth grazing the veins on her neck. But what has come back most vividly is the memory of Sherlock Holmes pointing a shotgun directly at her as Count Dracula used her limp body as a human shield.

That she was delirious from loss of blood, exposure to the elements, and nearly in shock does not seem to matter. If she had a clear and complete memory of that night, I'm sure she would feel the same way I did—gratitude and relief that we made it through the episode with a minimum of harm. Mary now believes that Holmes wanted her dead in order to clear the way for my returning to Baker Street. She is unmoved by the fact that it was Holmes, not she, who was savaged by one of Dracula's wolves. (That I took a wolf bite myself on her behalf seems to matter little.) She refuses to accept that Holmes is an exceptional marksman and would not have harmed her had he pulled the trigger, and I do not believe he would have done if it meant Mary would come to harm.

Which brings us full circle to the strongest delusion Mary sustained while under Dracula's spell—that I prefer Holmes' society to hers. This just isn't true; if staying at Baker Street had meant that much to me, would I have married her in the first place? I am the first to admit that when Holmes is on the scent and his swift, precise mind is in flight, I am filled with wonder and admiration. Indeed, who is not?

But it takes a strong and peculiar constitution to live the life of Sherlock Holmes. He does not need the succor of a feminine caress, nor does he seek the comfort and warmth of family life. As the last of my line, I want these things. I want to share my adventures with a son, pass my knowledge and experiences on to the next generation, so all that I am, and the modest part I have played in the world's grand drama, does not vanish in the dust when I am gone. (I am under no illusion that my writings will linger beyond the usual year or so it takes a book to complete its print run.) The challenge of a puzzle and the strains of a violin may be enough for Holmes, but it could never sustain me for long.

Last week we had one row too many, and Mary, as she always does, retreated to the wilds of the Pentangeli, the Cecil Forrester estate in Winchester. I was alone. I had lit a cigar, poured a whiskey, and was about to settle in for an evening's reading when the curtain rustled. Startled, I leapt to my feet and balled my fists, only to drop them when the nervous figure of Sherlock Holmes stepped into my parlor.

"Holmes! How did you get in here?"

"You really ought to have better locks on your windows," said my jumpy friend. "After you hear what I have to say, you shall surely need them."

I noticed right away that his hand was bleeding, and, over his protests, I fetched my medical kit. The wounds were not serious, just some lacerations to the knuckles, but they went rather deep. Once the hand was bandaged, I offered Holmes a chair and poured a glass. Holmes positioned the chair so that he could keep an eye on the window.

"Of course you recall our sojourn in Castle Dracula," he said.

"With horror," said I, "but Mina Harker assures me that the count is dead. What could this have to do with him?"

Holmes made a dismissive gesture. He was dressed in a workman's dark clothing, and his features were obscured by a black cloth cap, which he removed and twisted in his hands as he spoke. If at all possible, he looked paler and thinner than usual. His hair, never thick to begin with, stuck up in thin little tufts from long hours under his cap. Though the curtains were drawn, his eyes kept darting to the window, as if it might implode at any moment. Becoming wary myself, I locked the parlor door and turned the lamp down.

"A wise precaution, Watson. You will soon find me a very dangerous guest."

"Tell me." I found a notebook and took copious notes, with which I shall flesh out this account at some future date. What I put down here is a rough recollection, as my notes are back in London.

"You may remember that first night in the castle, when I discovered the plot hatched by Count Dracula and Professor Moriarty to take over Barings Brothers in the wake of the Argentine loan crisis."

I nodded.

"On our return, I contacted Mycroft right away and shared my suspicions. Fortunately, there were plenty of men in the financial world who felt as nervous about Argentine loans as did we, and so Mycroft was able to pull some strings from his headquarters at the Diogenes Club to undercut Moriarty's move, so that when Barings fell, the Bank of England stepped in to catch them."

"Imagine the uproar if the public were to find out," I

said. "I trust your brother is keeping the affair properly bottled up?"

Holmes nodded and continued, "Moriarty lost millions, and his fortune was in jeopardy from Inland Revenue. It seemed that, at last, I was about to bring him to ground.

"It is no shame on my part to say I underestimated the good professor. He had prepared for such a disaster, and so when the blow fell, his name was not so much as whispered."

"But he held you responsible."

"Properly so. I have spent the months since setting the stage for the final curtain. But the man is the Napoleon of crime, and for my every attack on one flank he dodges me on another. I know his every move and he knows mine. But the genius of the thing is that he places enough walls between himself and his misdeeds so that I can never directly connect him to anything I know he has done. Until now.

"You see, Watson, the greatest hindrance in the life of a criminal is insecurity. He is always looking over his shoulder; he is never quite safe. And even Professor Moriarty, genius and master of mathematics though he may be, cannot think of everything. So one of his thieves drops a telling detail during questioning by Lestrade. A footprint is found where it should not be. Two different kinds of cigarette ash turn up at what should have been a one-man burglary. And so, over time, the painting is limned in clearer and clearer detail, and, as the pursuit continues, Moriarty finds that he must be ever more careful.

"But I must confess an element of enjoyment at our

intellectual thrust and parry. That he is capable of engineering a murder over a hundred miles away is appalling; but that he is able to do it inspires a reluctant sense of awe. This is where I must confess my own flaws; my horror at his crimes was lost in my admiration at his skill.

"But at last he made a trip—only a little, little trip—but it was more than he could afford, when I was so close upon him. I had my chance, and, starting from that point, I have woven my net round him until now it is all ready to close. In three days—that is to say, on Monday next—matters will be ripe, and the professor, with all the principal members of his gang, will be in the hands of the police. Then will come the greatest criminal trial of the century, the clearing up of over forty mysteries, and the rope for all of them; but if we move at all prematurely, you understand, they may slip out of our hands even at the last moment."

"But?"

"Moriarty surprised me once again by abandoning all pretense of subtlety and visiting me in my quarters not two nights ago."

"Extraordinary!"

O to have been present for that encounter, the meeting of two brilliant and nimble intellects, the one bent in the tenacious pursuit of justice, the other on greed and destruction. We knew his features already, of course; Holmes even photographed him once, but this was insufficient preparation to greet the man in the flesh. Holmes described the good professor as a cornered reptile, a reflection of his black-hearted soul. Holmes places Moriarty's age at about fifty-five. Almost as tall and thin and pale as Holmes, Moriarty's prominent skull domes out in a white curve, and his two black eyes are deeply sunken in his head. Ever the mathematics scholar, Moriarty's shoulders are rounded from much study, and his face protrudes forward and, in an odd trait, his head constantly oscillates from side to side, so that he is always taking in a wide view. During this singular interview, Holmes said, Moriarty left the door open and stood only a step away.

Holmes quietly slipped his revolver from the drawer and slipped it into his dressing-gown. Moriarty was not fooled; Holmes placed his weapon on the table within instant reach.

"You have less frontal development than I should have expected," he told Holmes. "This duel of ours really must end. It can have but one outcome, you see."

"And it will play out on Monday."

"How long have we been at this, Mr. Holmes? Over and over, your *attaque au fer* is met with my riposte. I feint, you parry. We have pinked one another too many times."

"So you consider yourself 'pinked' after the Barings affair? Admirable."

"And it is the reason we have come to this crisis. The situation is becoming an impossible one. It is necessary that you should withdraw. You have worked things in such a fashion that we have only one resource left. It has been an intellectual treat to me to see the way in which you have grappled with this affair, and I say, unaffectedly, that it would be a grief to me to be forced to take any extreme measure. You smile, sir, but I assure you that it really would."

"I must confess, Professor, that I share a similar admiration. But that pales when I consider how many fortunes lost and lives ruined from your enterprises. The net is drawn and you are ensnared. One way or another in a few days you will lose all."

"You hope to place me in the dock. I tell you that I will never stand in the dock. If you are clever enough to bring destruction upon me, rest assured that I shall do as much to you."

"If I were assured of the former eventuality I would, in the interests of the public, cheerfully accept the latter," replied Holmes.

"I can promise you the one, but not the other," snarled Moriarty, who then turned his rounded back on Holmes and slithered back to his den.

Holmes has been on the run since; after our interview, Holmes told me later, they even set fire to 221B, but it was put out before anything of importance was lost. There is now but one way for Moriarty to retain his liberty, and that is with the death of Mr. Sherlock Holmes. Two attempts have been made on his life thus far, and my heart filled with fear as the proudest man I have ever known crouched like a frightened fox in the dark shadows of my parlor.

We laid plans. The difficulty in trying to outthink someone like Moriarty is that you can run circles around yourself trying to anticipate every possibility, in the end inducing intellectual paralysis. One thing we knew for certain: that we were being watched. Rather than try to outfox them here, we decided we would have better luck doing so in unfamiliar surroundings. Let Moriarty believe he has anticipated our every move.

We laid out an elaborate plan to rendezvous at Victoria Station. Mycroft Holmes was drafted as a cab driver, which caused his brother no small amount of mirth; it may be the first time Mycroft has seen daylight in years. While I followed Holmes' instructions to the letter, he still managed to surprise me, joining me in the guise of an aged, ailing Italian priest.

We managed to dodge Moriarty at Canterbury, where we sent our luggage on a fine holiday in Paris, and took ourselves off to Dieppe, and from there to our current location, in Brussels.

The Strasbourg sun is rising slowly behind my back as I write this, and with it bright rays of hope that by this time tomorrow, Professor Moriarty and his gang will firmly and safely behind bars so that Holmes and I can return to London.

I can hear Holmes' impatient and steady tread in the room next door, the air thickening with shag as the hour approaches when Inspector Gregson should be behind his desk, awaiting Holmes' wire.

It is only fitting, pitted as we are against the Napoleon of crime, that Holmes and I should find ourselves in Belgium yesterday, spending a fine spring day touring the battlefield at Waterloo, about eleven miles or so south of Brussels. It was here, of course, that the Duke of Wellington with bravery, pluck, and good British common sense outmaneuvered the Emperor Napoleon and forever spared Europe the nightmare of permanent French domination. Future tyrants, I am sure, will look back on this battle and think twice before pulling the British lion's tail.

Today, of course, the battlefield is tranquil, rolling green ridges with the countryside dotted with the sienna roofs and whitewashed walls of medieval villages and lazy country farms. Were it not for the war memorials that crop up at random like granite copses all over the battle-field, one might never know this land ever hosted any-thing more threatening than scarecrows. I hold particular ire for the Lion's Mount monument to the Dutch Prince of Orange. While I am sure he performed with great courage, the bit of shrapnel he took in the arse did not jus-tify tearing up several acres of the Allied side of the battle-field to put up that gaudy statue, though I must admit I admired the panoramic view from its heights this morn-ing.

Holmes and I spent the afternoon prowling the farm at Hougoumont, which proved so crucial to Napoleon's defeat. A crumbling chateau wall brought back to mind some of the decay and disintegration of Castle Dracula, though it is not nearly as old. I ran my palm lightly across the bullet-pocked bricks, wondering whether the original owners had been nobles forced out in the Revolution, or if spots of brave British blood marked the dirty whitewash along the exterior wall, or if those stains were nothing more than the dust and rain of nearly eighty years.

The bullet holes and monuments, the battle that Holmes and I were quietly engaged in, suddenly brought back memories of Maiwand with great force. I recollect vividly the bloody day the Afghan hordes pushed us back. The Afghans outnumbered us ten to one, intense heat and thirst had drained our spirits, and the bloody, ragtag rem-nants of the other companies flooded our position in their panicked retreat, obliterating any chain of command and forcing us out into the open, naked to enemy fire. We made for the ravine at Khig, beyond which lay water, med-icine, and ammunition. I was too busy for fighting. Our civilian drivers had fled, and it was up to myself, my man Murray, and any soldier I outranked to sling the wounded onto carts and get them off the battlefield.

To me fell the task of distinguishing who should be taken and who not; to my dying day I'll not forget the young soldier, perhaps twenty years old at most, lying on his side, his hand outstretched and his features aglow in relief at the sight of a doctor. But his tunic was soaked in oozing black blood, and I saw a bit of large intestine protruding from the smoldering fabric of his uniform. As I sadly shook my head and passed him by, the very life drained from his pleading brown eyes, and the light faded, a youthful candle snuffed out. Glowing hope had faded to disappointment, horror and shock at the last.

I could not afford tears at the time, but now the vivid recollection dampened by eyes. At such times I tell myself that it was not I who put them in that position, not I who decided who should live and who should die. That choice was made by Afghan gunners, and I believe I did the very best I could with my poor powers as bullets whizzed past my ears. I blotted out the screams of the dying for the sake of the living.

But even that was taken from me when a Jezail bullet clipped me soundly in the shoulder; to this day I can't tell what happened to my leg. Murray pulled me clear and dumped me on a cart before I could protest.

Later. When I reminisced about this to Holmes (who has made much study of such matters while examining corpses at Bart's) he told me that as bullets are made of lead, they are not the solid little metal balls we think them to be. Lead bullets are soft and malleable; they fragment on contact sometimes, and on striking bone will ricochet in the body, resulting in some unusual wounds. After taking a look at my scars, Holmes felt it was very probable that the bullet which hit me split on hitting the scapula (most likely on the mass of bone that is the coracoid process), bouncing back out and lodging in my leg. I know there was an operation to remove the bullet later, but I never saw it and don't know what happened to the bullet. Likely, there are fragments in my body still.

All this was racing in my mind when Holmes approached me.

"Perhaps we shouldn't have come today," he remarked, handing me a welcome cigarette. "This is supposed to be a pleasant respite, and it's brought you back to Afghanistan."

"How did you—"

"It's in your eyes, my dear Watson. Your war memories always register the same expression."

"Would that we had a Wellington at Maiwand. Things might have turned out differently. 'The battle at Maiwand was won on the playing fields of Eton.' Has a nice ring to it, don't you think?"

"The Battle of Waterloo was won not on the playing fields of Eton, but by Belgian insubordination," said Holmes. "You see, Watson, as at Maiwand, the British thoroughly misread the situation. Wellington always believed in keeping a clear route to the sea open in case retreat was necessary, never mind how far inland his army happened to be. Add to this the fact that his information was roughly half a day behind actual events. Wellington thought the French would advance from the southwest of Brussels, so he gave orders to the Dutch and Belgian forces to concentrate at Nivelles, not knowing Napoleon had the village of Quatre-Bras in his sights.

"But the Dutch and Belgians, unjustly maligned by you, knew the local terrain quite a bit better and realized that Wellington's plan put too great a distance between his army and the Prussians under General Blucher. Wellington would have opened the gates wide for Napoleon. So Orange's generals ignored Wellington's orders and concentrated their forces at Quatre-Bras, which delayed the French and toppled a distinctly different set of history's dominoes. Napoleon made a number of mistakes of his own, like putting his brother in charge of the force that kept attacking this farm. But I'll leave that discussion for another time."

"Come Monday we'll both be in better moods, I expect," said I. "Is it not fitting, Holmes, that as we tour Waterloo, the Napoleon of crime is about to meet his own?"

"I am confident, but not fully confident," admitted Holmes. "We both know what is at stake, and we both know where the blow will fall. I can only hope I have successfully anticipated and parried Moriarty's every possible counter-move. In the meantime, let us enjoy the sunshine, our repast *al fresco*, and hope your Wellingtonian metaphor proves to be apt."

Later. Once again, everything has changed, and I must be brief. We are in flight for our lives once more.

Holmes telegraphed Scotland Yard this morning, and we spent the day exploring Strasbourg. We found a reply waiting for us at our hotel on our return in the evening. Holmes tore it open, and then with a bitter curse hurled it into the grate.

"I might have known it!" he groaned. "Moriarty has escaped! They have secured the whole gang with the exception of him and one or two others. Of course, when I had left the country there was no one to cope with him, but I did think that I had put the game in their hands. I think that you had better return to England, Watson."

"Why?"

"Because you will find me a dangerous companion now."

"You already were."

"I have taken his fortune, and now his organisation. Moriarty is lost if he returns to London. He has nothing to devote his energies to save revenging himself upon me. He said as much in our short interview, and I fancy that he meant it. I should certainly recommend you to return to your practice."

It was hardly an appeal to be successful with one who was an old campaigner as well as an old friend. Besides, I have reasons of my own to continue. We sat in the Strasbourg salle-a-manger arguing the question for half an hour, but the time has come to pack. Holmes has not told me where we are going; I expect that decision will be made at the station.

May 3, 1891

But for the constant glances over our shoulders and the intense scrutiny we pay every falling rock, I believe I would be having one of the finest holidays of my life.

To-day we settled in at the Englischer Hof in the Swiss Alpine village of Meiringen. Peter Steiler the elder, our landlord, speaks excellent English, having served for three years as waiter at the Grosvenor Hotel in London.

"What suggestions do you have for a pair of aimless wanderers?" Holmes asked.

"Springtime is delightful in the Alps, Mr. Holmes," replied Steiler. "You can spend a day hiking the hills, where you will find the village of Rosenlaui. Getting there will take most of the day if you dawdle and enjoy the view, and the inn is most accommodating.

"If you don't mind a short break from your route, you will also pass the Reichenbach Falls, which are never more impressive than at this time of the year. The stream is nearly brimming with melted snow, and I can promise you a spectacular display of nature's power and beauty."

"Just the thing!" Holmes cried with delight.

After we settled in, we wandered into the village and found a pub serving excellent Swiss beer and hearty Tyrolean cuisine. Holmes seemed content, almost at peace.

"You're contemplating retirement, aren't you?" I said at last.

"Once Moriarty meets his fate," said he, "my detecting career will have reached its pinnacle. Without him, much of the challenge will be gone; Lestrade is mastering the rudiments of deduction at last, and passing them to his colleagues; and my labours on the Continent earlier this year have left me well enough off so that I never again need to take a problem to appease Mrs. Hudson.

"If my record were closed to-night I could still survey it with equanimity. The air of London is the sweeter for my presence. In over a thousand cases I am not aware that I have ever used my powers upon the wrong side. Of late I have been tempted to look into the problems furnished by nature rather than those more superficial ones for which our artificial state of society is responsible. Your memoirs will draw to an end, Watson, upon the day that I crown my career by the capture or extinction of the most dangerous and capable criminal in Europe."

"I shall cherish those days to the end of my own, Holmes," said I, and we clinked our mugs together.

My heart will be heavy on Friday, for I can neglect my practice no longer. Serenity does not come easily to Sherlock Holmes, and his mood tonight will linger with me to the last.

CHAPTER ELEVEN:
THE REICHENBACH FALLS

Dr. Watson's Journal

May 5, 1891

O bitterness, failure and despair! Sherlock Holmes is dead, and there is now a great, aching void in my heart, for it is I who am to blame. Without me, Moriarty would never have known where he needed to be, would never have found the ideal spot to work his malevolent will on the fate of Sherlock Holmes.

Now that it has happened, so much is clear. I realize now that Holmes had foreseen his fate, and resolved to accept it with calm and composure; indeed, it was at the uppermost of his mind as we left London. If only he had shared with me what he knew, given me the chance to talk him out of it, maybe all might yet be well.

But Holmes himself planted the seed when he quoted Moriarty as using the words "inevitable destruction" to finish their battle. All along, he had known it would end this way.

How many times have I seen it? How many dying patients have had that same air of peaceful calm as their mortal days wane, and their work on earth is done? How many have shared their pastoral visions of Elysium while their hearts slow, and then stop? How could I have been so blind?

Now, the happiest holiday I have had since my honeymoon ends with funeral preparations. The bodies were recovered this morning. I personally examined Holmes: his expression slack, his skin cold and pallid, no heartbeat, no breath, likely cause of death a blow to the skull sustained while falling onto the Reichenbach's rocks; there is a slight indentation behind the left ear. Holmes was dead before he hit the water; this explains the lack of water when I pressed his torso to determine if he had drowned.

I give not a damn what happens to Moriarty's body, but Mycroft Holmes telegraphed his instructions this morning, and they shall be carried out to the letter.

But first I must record the events that led to the tragic demise of Sherlock Holmes. My tears have run their course, and I must force myself to proceed, while the details are still fresh in my mind.

One day I will share this story with the world, should I ever bring myself to publicly admit the truth: that I was as much Moriarty's marionette as surely as if I'd had strings attached to my limbs.

Holmes maintained his cheery demeanour as we set out at about ten o'clock. By early afternoon, we had made our way to the Reichenbach Falls, actually the Upper Reichenbach Falls. Years of carving by nature have created a channel of jagged black rock down which roar powerful cascades of water, swollen by the spring snowmelt, that plunge 300 feet or so to a tremendous black abyss below and a dark pool of unknown depth, the vast endless spray creating permanent rainbows in the sunlight—a magnificent sight that will forever hold a bitter memory for me now.

On we climbed up the path which has been carved through the rock to the top in order to afford travellers a full view, but it is a narrow path; the only way in is also the only way out. We stood silently, Holmes and I. I took in the majestic view; the top of the Reichenbach looks over towering snowcapped Alpine mountains, rich and green fields and forests, and the ancient glaciers that feed the flowing waters.

For his part, Holmes was leaning on his Alpine-stock, scanning the rock face and looking like nothing so much as a hawk soaring over the fields looking for prey. Not for him the magnificent power and beauty of Nature this day; I now realize he was looking to join the battle. We stood wordless for several minutes, when I heard my name being bellowed by a young Swiss lad who ran panting up the path. He handed me a note in Steiler's hand, claiming that an Englishwoman had fallen ill at the hotel, and was demanding to see an English doctor.

"Perhaps she doesn't speak German, Watson," Holmes said on reading the note. "Surely yours are the most capable hands any of our countrymen could request in times of crisis. By all means, attend to the poor lady."

"Holmes, remember why we are here."

"It has never left my mind, dear fellow, I assure you. Our young companion here seems to be worried about his father. Perhaps I can be of assistance to him. I'll tarry here a little longer and meet you this evening in Rosenlaui."

How bland a parting, especially in light of what I know now. I need hardly go into detail here about what must surely be obvious: the note turned out to be fraudulent. Steiler told me it had been written by a tall, bald Englishman who couldn't keep his head still—add master of forgery to Moriarty's endless list of sinister talents. It took more than two hours, but, my chest huffing like a locomotive, I made it back to the top of the Reichenbach Falls.

Holmes' Alpine-stock still leaned against the boulder at which I had last seen him standing, sending a chill to my heart that had nothing to do with the cool and moist Alpine air. The young Swiss lad vanished as well; a Moriarty stooge, no doubt. One of the small, lingering niggles is Holmes' comment about the boy being worried about his father. Perhaps Holmes detected some sort of hold Moriarty had over the man. Or perhaps he was simply a local rustic in need of a few easy *schillings*.

It took me a moment to come to my senses, so overwhelmed was I at the horror. Surely Holmes would know what to do; and so I made my attempt.

Holmes' admonitions about observation and deduction vivid in my mind, I followed the path to the scene of the battle. The impressions in the earth, the broken saplings, scrapings on the rocks, told the whole story.

Moriarty was more than Holmes' intellectual equal; he must have also been Holmes' physical equal as well, deceptively strong and quick. Holmes was adept at boxing and fencing, but in the mud was writ someone tripping over a tree root. I recognized a body contour, with a deep impression from a knee near the right ribs. A piece of the bank gave way just above the fall. The mortal enemies were struggling at the bank when it collapsed, and they both hurtled to their doom over the black rocks into the maelstrom far below.

Yet I still have one final word from Sherlock Holmes, who had rested his staff on top of his silver cigarette case. When I picked it up, a small square of paper fluttered to

the ground, three pages from his notebook and the note which lays on the desk before me and roils my heart.
"MY DEAR WATSON:

"I write these few lines through the courtesy of Mr. Moriarty, who awaits my convenience for the final discussion of those questions which lie between us. He has been giving me a sketch of the methods by which he avoided the English police and kept himself informed of our movements. They certainly confirm the very high opinion which I had formed of his abilities. I am pleased to think that I shall be able to free society from any further effects of his presence, though I fear that it is at a cost which will give pain to my friends, and especially, my dear Watson, to you.

"In particular, it pains me to report that Moriarty never lost track of us. As we toured the battlefield at Waterloo, I spotted the unmistakable silhouette of Col. Sebastian Moran, who, as you know, serves as Moriarty's chief of staff. Bold as day, he was leaning against the Orange monument, following us with his binoculars as if we were a pair of prize antelope grazing on the plains of the Serengeti. But I knew he, or one of his underlings, would be there, for while we were on the train to Brussels, I spotted more than one porter peering into his hat. It was the simplest of matters to investigate this unusual occurrence; I arranged to bump into one of them when the train lurched, dislodging his headgear. Your photo was nestled in the lining. Moriarty had seemingly bribed every porter in Europe to keep an eye out for you. In my arrogance, I assumed it was not necessary to disguise you; indeed, I shame myself to have endangered you in this manner. I should have sent you home there and then. But had I done so, the game would have been exposed, and Moriarty's reign would never end. In any event, who better than you, my dearest, stalwart friend, to make sure that the ends of this affair are neatly and properly tied?

"I have already explained to you that my career had in any case reached its crisis, and that no possible conclusion to it could be more congenial to me than this.

"Indeed, if I may make a full confession to you, I was quite convinced that the letter from Meiringen was a hoax, and I allowed you to depart on that errand under the persuasion that some development of this sort would follow. Tell Inspector Patterson that the papers which he needs to convict the gang are in pigeonhole M., done up in a blue envelope and inscribed 'Moriarty.' I made every disposition of my property before leaving England and handed it to my brother Mycroft. Pray give my greetings to the kind-hearted and forgiving Mrs. Watson, and believe me to be, my dear fellow,

"Very sincerely yours,
"SHERLOCK HOLMES."

The local constabulary have confirmed my observations, and now I have the sad duty of bringing my friend's body back to London.

CHAPTER TWELVE: THE FUNERAL OF SHERLOCK HOLMES

May 9, 1891

Sherlock Holmes has returned to God.

To accommodate Mycroft Holmes, the memorial service was held at a chapel near the Diogenes Club. He maintained a tight, firm hand over the whole affair, and only a very few were allowed to attend.

I was pleased that Mycroft agreed to burying Holmes in the city, rather than some little-visited family tomb in the country. If Holmes is not buried in London, I should rarely be able to visit him; neither could Mycroft.

I believe Holmes would have approved of his brother's choice of chapel; it is dark and intimate, lit by sunshine streaming through a stained glass history of the Crusades and Christianity. Mary and I took a seat close to the front, next to my one-time dresser Stamford, who introduced me to Holmes ten years ago. We have not kept in close touch since then; I have sometimes seen him at the Criterion Bar or at Simpson's, and on those occasions when I visit Bart's.

"I've hardly seen Holmes since he moved his laboratory to Baker Street," said he, after I introduced my wife. "It's as if my sole purpose in God's plan was to bring you two together. I have greatly enjoyed your chronicles, Watson; that's why I came today."

"You will forever have my thanks," I replied. "Where would any of us be without him?"

Mrs. Hudson arrived shortly and joined us. Among the other mourners, I spotted the hereditary King of Bohemia himself, Wilhelm Gottsreich Sigismund von Ormstein, once again failing at incognito. It was gratifying to see Helen Stoner, whom we saved from a vicious swamp adder, not to mention an equally vile stepfather, and Sir Henry Baskerville, who must have crossed the Atlantic from Canada in record time. Inspectors Gregson, Lestrade and Patterson represented Scotland Yard. Dr. Conan Doyle came as well; I am meeting him soon to discuss the best venue for publishing my memoirs.

Of course, the late Irene Adler is missed; she is the only woman for whom Holmes ever held a soft spot in his heart. We never solved her mysterious death.

Yet, save the massive Mycroft, nowhere did I spot anyone recognizably from the Holmes family.

Once the vicar concluded his remarks, Mycroft took the lectern. Usually an imposing man, to-day the weight of his grief seemed to settle into his shoulders and diminish him. Indeed, we are all a little lesser now.

"You will forgive our family, I hope, for having said goodbye to Sherlock in a separate service this morning," Mycroft said. "But those of you whose lives he has touched, those of you whose lives he has saved, deserve your own farewell. For you gave purpose to his life. He could have entered government service, as have I; he could have devoted his genius to medicine, or music, or chemistry.

"Instead, he chose to apply his matchless abilities to the detection and eradication of crime, treating this endeavour as a science and art, rather than as a trade. In doing this, Sherlock changed the world, for now the criminal can no longer conduct his work unseen in the dark. If he smoked a cigar, left a footprint, or even a single thread of cloth, he can now be caught. How often has Sherlock Holmes amazed us by telling each detail of our lives on a moment's acquaintance? How many villains came to justice because my brother was able to give a precise description after a few minutes alone with magnifying glass and measuring tape? I see the Scotland Yard delegation nodding; the number must be considerable, indeed.

"Dr. John Watson, the world owes you its thanks as well. For had you not shared Sherlock's adventures, it might have taken years for his methods to catch up with the constabulary. Though he had his quarrels with the way you told your tales, he was certainly indebted to you for the results. Through your writings, the man and his methods will live far longer than the seven-and-thirty short years we were privileged to have him on this earth. Farewell, my brother, and my friend."

My poor pen is barely adequate to convey the power of his words. Around me, eyes glistened, and handkerchiefs dabbed at them. It took a moment for me to gather my thoughts, and I took my place before the assemblage, keeping my voice as even as I could.

"Thank you, Mr. Holmes, for your kind words. I, too, know the unbearable pain of losing a brother. Now I have lost my closest friend, my dearest companion, the best and wisest man whom I have ever known. I feel that loss keenly, for had my own wits been as sharp as his, had I been thinking as clearly as I should have, had I not been duped, I should not be standing here today to share your grief.

"I never sought literary garlands, nor did either Holmes or myself ever quest for fame, fortune and glory.

Indeed, what appears in the public prints is often so far from the truth that I felt compelled to set the record straight. If, in the course of this, we have brought benefits to those I see before me, I am thankful.

"But we are here for different purposes, you and I. You come to pay tribute to the man who delivered you from danger and difficulty. I am here to atone. I have let him down, and that will be on my heart for eternity."

Trembling, I took my seat next to Stamford, who squeezed my arm in sympathy. The service soon concluded and we pallbearers—Mycroft, Stamford, Reginald Musgrave, Lestrade, Victor Trevor, and myself—loaded the casket into the hearse. It seemed lighter than it should have to me. Perhaps Mycroft shouldered a heavier load than the rest of us.

The burial service was brief, almost perfunctory. The memorial exhausted us all, and I, at least, had no tears left. Once the vicar finished and Mycroft threw the first handful of earth onto the coffin, we began to drift away.

Since then, I have had a note from Mycroft, requesting me not to undertake a biography of my friend. He feels that the two narratives I have thus far published are enough.

But I will not let Holmes' memory die. If Mycroft objects to a formal biography, I shall respect his wishes. My own recollections are a different matter. I have published my reminiscences before and shall again. I still have my notes from our cases, and, of course, this journal.

Holmes may be gone, but he will not be forgotten. Mycroft be damned! The tales of how we averted a scandal that threatened the king of Bohemia; the terrifying Hound of the Baskervilles; the singular case of the Red-

Headed League; Hugh Boone and his twisted lip; the bizarre tale of Violet Hunter, and all the others, should be laid before the public so that the world can see what it has lost in that keen and remarkable mind, and that well-hidden, but empathetic, heart.

CHAPTER THIRTEEN: THE FARRINGDON STREET GHOUL

Dr. Watson's Journal

June 12, 1891

It seems that my life with crime has not ended, after all.

At about four this morning Mary and I were awakened by a furious pounding at the door. Fearing an emergency, I donned my dressing-gown and found an anxious Lestrade, his ferret-like face tight with fear, standing in the fog.

"I'm sorry to bother you, Doctor, but you're the closest physician," the inspector said. "Come quickly! We may have another Ripper!"

I donned clothing as quickly as I could, grabbed my bag, and followed Lestrade into a waiting hansom.

"What happened?" I asked.

"There's a dead drab in an alley on Upper Thames Street," he said. "Her name's Deborah Burke, age about three-and-forty, whored herself for gin and a flop. One of the other girls saw her head into her usual alley with a customer, then she heard Deborah scream. Another man ran into the alley."

Lestrade paused.

"And then?" I prompted.

"And no one came out. Damnedest thing. You'll see what I mean when we get there."

"If the victim is dead, then what do you need me for?"

"To officially determine the cause and manner of death and to put some of that knowledge you've gleaned from Mr. Holmes to good use."

"Now, Lestrade, really, I'm not a detective, as Holmes so frequently reminded me."

"You were with him for nigh on ten years and the three of us have examined God knows how many bodies. I cannot believe you haven't picked up something. If the Ripper's back, then every second counts."

Upper Thames Street is a gray, grimy loathsome neighborhood near the wharves, den of addicts, prostitutes, and thieves. Indeed, I found Holmes in disguise there once while he was investigating a case.

Two constables blocked the entrance of a grimy alley, beyond which I could see the corpse. The stench of blood, dirt and filth struck me at once; when we lit the lanterns, rats scattered.

A horrific sight greeted me when the pale yellow glow passed over the body, but there was one reason to breathe easy; this was not the work of Jack the Ripper.

"How do you know?" asked Lestrade. "He was caught in the act. There wasn't time to finish."

"Take a look," said I, kneeling and preparing for my examination. "Bring the lamp a little closer. You can see the slash across the neck goes from left to right. Whoever did this took her from behind and was right-handed. As you know very well, Lestrade, the Ripper was left-handed."

It was, of course, Holmes who originally pointed that out to me when we were called into the case in 1888. I am certain Holmes knew who the scoundrel was, but he never told me, and the case remains officially unsolved to this very day.

This victim, as Lestrade had told me, was about forty-three years old, and destined to die of cirrhosis had she not been attacked. On further examination, I found more than one wound; a large, deep gash was visible near the jugular, as well as a couple of other wounds in the same general area, likely inflicted by the knife used to make the fatal incision. The rest of the body was unviolated, except by venereal disease. The wounds were so severe that she must have bled to death in minutes.

"If you need a cause of death, it is from blood loss resulting from the throat being slashed," I told Lestrade. "There is no doubt of murder, but it is not the work of Jack the Ripper. Perhaps the work of a similar madman, but at least not that one."

"That is somewhat comforting," the detective said.

Too late, I thought about footprints, and how Holmes would have chastised me for disturbing the scene. Now it was overrun. In any event, the fog was as thick as molasses. It would have been easy for someone to slip away.

"Any idea who the passerby was?" I asked.

Lestrade consulted his notebook. "About six feet tall, lean, pale, dressed in black, face covered by a cloth cap, according to Mrs. Jensen."

"What about the knife?"

"We searched the alley and didn't find it."

By now, the sun had broken the city skyline and soon we wouldn't need lamps to examine the scene. Though my work was done, this case aroused my curiosity, and I wondered if, in my own meagre fashion, I might successfully apply Holmes' methods.

But it was hopeless. Between the police search of the alley and my own examination, there were no useful footprints. The body lay where it fell ...

"By Jove!" I cried. "There are no signs of a third party! I see no evidence of a scuffle, Lestrade, do you? Are you sure this passerby tried to intervene?"

"What do you mean, Watson?"

"Just this: Suppose the passerby was an accomplice. That they both meant to murder this woman for some reason."

"Did anyone see the villains leave?"

The constables shook their heads. "Too dark, too much fog," Brock said.

"That may be a line of inquiry for you, Lestrade."

"My hat is off to you, Mr. Holmes," Lestrade replied with a touch of gentle mockery. "You were a good student after all. I am relieved to know we don't have a reincarnated Ripper on our hands. Thank you, Doctor. We can take it from here. You'll be available for the inquest?"

"Of course."

June 15, 1891

When I returned from my afternoon rounds, the maid handed me a note asking me to call Lestrade on the telephone.

"Good news, Doctor. We have apprehended our killer from last Friday."

"Good work, Lestrade. How did it happen?"

"He picked up Emily Shawe last night and asked her for a favour she wouldn't agree to. He offered her a locket that Emily recognized as belonging to Deborah Burke.

She screamed for a constable, and he pulled a knife. Luckily, one of our men was nearby, and made the arrest. We just got his confession."

"Who is he?"

"He's a German sailor, name of Ebberling. Seems he likes to spend his shore leave crawling pubs and chasing whores, like so many of 'em do."

"What about the accomplice?"

"Nothing there, Doctor. Ebberling says he'd never seen the man before in his life. They argued; this other man was apparently quite strong, because Ebberling says he was tossed away, light as a feather, back to the end of the alley. He crawled away so nobody would see him."

There seemed to be something else, and I pressed for more.

"It's about this other man," said Lestrade. "I think he was in one of the pubs last night. A fight had broken out, and Johnson and Rance went in to quell it. A shouting match over something trivial erupted into a brawl, the whole place was soon in turmoil, and at one point someone smashed a bottle on the bar and went after another man with it.

"The blood was flowing freely, and a couple of the witnesses saw a man dressed in black, cloth cap pulled over his eyes, scoop up a glass, grab one of the victims, and squeeze the wound in an attempt to fill the glass. No one tried to stop this in the melee, and once the glass was full, the victim was dropped and our man disappeared."

"I don't know what to make of that, Lestrade."

"I don't know, either. There's nothing particularly illegal about it, but it is certainly strange. If this man was also in the alley with Miss Burke, was he also after her blood? And why would anybody be after anyone else's blood?"

"The only man I know in London with that sort of expertise," I said, "is Dr. John Seward. He runs the Holloway House asylum in Purfleet."

"Thank you, Dr. Watson," Lestrade said, and rang off.

EDITORIAL INTERLUDE

It's now time to give Dr. Watson a break and let one of his colleagues take over.* Dr. Seward takes the story over for a while from here.

Holmes and Watson returned from Castle Dracula late in August 1890. By this time, Count Dracula had largely left the financial scheming to Professor Moriarty and embarked on his true reason for coming to England: hunting fresh supplies of blood. I know that Sherlock Holmes met with his brother Mycroft about a week later, presumably to discuss the coming Barings crisis, but the only record I have been able to find is a note in Holmes' datebook; what he and Mycroft actually discussed, I have no idea. All we know for sure was that the Bank of England stood ready as the lender of last resort when the blow finally fell in Argentina.

As *Dracula* readers know, Dr. John Seward ran a lunatic asylum that abutted Carfax, Dracula's English estate. Seward, along with Jonathan and Mina Harker, Dr. Van Helsing, Lord Godalming and Quincey Morris, drove Dracula from London on October 5, 1890, and they pursued him all the way back to Transylvania, catching up with him on November 8, within sight of Castle Dracula at twilight. Though Dracula's gipsy protectors battled the

---

* Again, I am indebted to the keen researchers at Hawkins, Harker, Graham & McFarlane for digging out and indexing the Seward, Harker and Godalming papers. —SS

band of vampire trackers from London, the Count was exposed in his coffin as the sun set near his castle. Had the shadows grown just a little bit longer a little bit sooner, Dracula might be with us yet. But Jonathan Harker and Quincey Morris between them were able to strike fatal blows with sharp knives, sending the villainous vampire to the dust. Morris sustained a fatal knife wound from one of the gipsies in the battle, but, according to Mina Harker, died thinking the sacrifice worth it.

Bram Stoker's account of the case was not to be published for another seven years, but word of what had happened circulated around London for some time, and Seward unintentionally became London's vampire expert once Van Helsing returned to Amsterdam; as the head of a mental hospital to boot, Seward was in an unusual position to learn of and evaluate vampire reports, and he received many strange requests. Certainly neither he, Lord Godalming nor Watson ever expected their paths to cross again, but fate has its ways ...

CHAPTER FOURTEEN:
OLD FEAR AND NEW LOVE

Dr. Seward's Diary

(dictation transcribed from wax cylinders)
June 15, 1891

Not a year has passed, and I am chasing vampires again. Twice today someone has asked me about vampire mania. This morning I received a visit from Dr. Archibald Stamford, resident at St. Bartholomew's.

"I wouldn't bother you ordinarily, but something strange has been happening at Bart's, and I think you might be able to shed some light," he said.

"How may I be of service?"

"Please tell me what you know of vampirism, and where I might find some literature on the subject."

He could find it on these very cylinders, but it will be years before those recordings see the light of day, if ever. The memories of my encounters with Count Dracula, and how he destroyed my poor beloved Lucy, gave me an involuntary shudder, still do. My heart will ever be with poor Arthur, who needed every ounce of his compassion and will to end her suffering. Had she accepted my proposal over his, I am not sure I could have struck the fatal blow that freed her in the end.

To the matter at hand. When Stamford gave me a curious glance, I rose and closed the window, even though the day was warm and pleasant.

"The world authority is Dr. Abraham Van Helsing, in Amsterdam," I replied. "I was his student, but ... why do you want to know?"

"There have been strange goings-on in the pathological wing, particularly in the morgue and some of the labs. Put succinctly, someone has been stealing blood."

"What?"

Stamford went on to explain that a lab attendant was seen draining blood from fresh corpses, and caught drinking it on one occasion. Not only that, students conducting blood research have found their supplies taken.

"Let's be clear," I said. "This man, so far as you are aware, has attacked no one?"

"No one living, though I wouldn't want to speak for his soul on Judgment Day. I should add that I have not seen him myself."

"He was draining the blood into a vessel."

"Yes."

"Not drinking directly from the corpse."

"As I told you."

This brought me great relief; a true vampire would not do these things.

"Without actually examining the patient, I would say your lab attendant suffers from religious mania, not vampirism," I said. "Vampires attack living victims and take their blood directly."

"Then why do you say this is religious mania?"

"Because your man is re-enacting Catholic rituals," I said. "Pouring blood into a cup is a literal way of tasting the blood of Christ. He may believe he is bringing himself closer to God in this deranged manner. Of course, this is pure conjecture. Without examining the patient, I can't be of any real help."

"Not a madman who believes he is a vampire, then?"

"Perhaps. I really need more information than this."

Stamford rose and extended his hand.

"Thank you, Doctor Seward, you've been most helpful. You have eased my mind somewhat."

When I returned from luncheon at around two, I found a Scotland Yard inspector waiting for me in my office. He was a short man, slender, with sharp weasel-like features, in age I should say about forty-five. He introduced himself as Inspector Lestrade.

"I have been told," he said, "that you know something of vampire mania."

"Not again," I said.

"What do you mean?"

I summarized the visit I had from Dr. Stamford, and asked Lestrade why he was here. He told the most extraordinary story about a man dressed in black who had been present at two violent crimes, and that he was seen draining blood into a glass at one of them.

"Could it be the same man?" asked Lestrade.

"I don't know. Dr. Stamford didn't describe this lab attendant to me. On the other hand, that there are two such people seems to strain coincidence."

"So such a man has not passed through your gates?"

"The last case we had that was remotely like this died last year," said I, thinking of the late Mr. Renfield. And, as with Stamford, I explained that this man, whoever he is, does not act like any vampire I have encountered. (I realize that two vampires do not an expert make, but still, it's two

more than most people ever encounter. And of those who
meet just one vampire, how many live to meet another?)

Lestrade did not ask me to elaborate; he thanked me
for my time, and left. I must write Van Helsing and see
what he thinks.

Later. At last, something cheerful to report. I have
received a note from Arthur Holmwood—he's Lord
Godalming now, I must remember that—formally
announcing his engagement to a Miss Amanda Keswick,
whose existence comes as a complete surprise to me. I have
not seen much of Arthur since our adventures with Count
Dracula last year, and I thought he would mourn Lucy
forever. After that ordeal, indeed, I should have thought
he would die a bachelor. This new love comes into his life
too soon for me to believe he fully knows what he is doing;
the mourning period for Lucy ended but two months ago.
Arthur is quite wealthy, and could be prey for a more common vampire—a "gold-digger," as the Americans say. I
shall form a fuller impression Saturday afternoon.

* * *

The Telegraph

June 18, 1891
POLICE SUSPECT GHOUL

A bloodthirsty madman is believed to be lurking on
the streets of London.

Inspector G. Lestrade of Scotland Yard seeks the public's assistance in identifying a man who intervened in a
brawl on Farringdon Street. Insp. Lestrade believes the
fight started in a dispute over cab fare. There have been
prior complaints about this cabman, the inspector said,

and he was recognized by some passersby who also had a dispute.

Before long, there was a melee in the street. Witnesses reported a tall man dressed in a black frock coat and cloth cap literally picking the brawlers up and tossing them aside like bags of grain. When he reached the cabman, who was bleeding from several wounds, he bent over him in what looked to onlookers like an attempt to minister to his wounds.

But in his statement to Insp. Lestrade, the cabman said the vile creature actually drank the blood pouring from his nose and cheeks. The ghoul has thin black hair, unusually sharp teeth, and foul breath. He did not inflict new harm, which comes as a puzzlement to police.

Insp. Lestrade said he knows of other incidents of this type, in which a man matching this description was seen stealing blood from crime and accident victims, sometimes drinking from a glass. If anyone knows who this man is, please contact Insp. Lestrade at once.

* * *

Dr. Seward's Diary

(dictation transcribed from wax cylinders)
June 20, 1891

I must say that Arthur has chosen a most beautiful and charming partner.

Miss Keswick is American, the daughter of an iron magnate. (Laughter) I must say, that sounds like a pun when it's spoken aloud. I must still be giddy from the champagne. What I meant to say is that her father, Mr. Eustace Keswick, was a miner who discovered iron ore in

Minnesota, struck a deal with U.S. Steel, and can now afford an English lord.

Did I just say that? I must be drunker than I thought. It's been such a long time since I've enjoyed any outright merry-making that its lack may be catching up to me all at once. This continues tomorrow. (Laughter, cut off suddenly.)

June 21, 1891

Oh, my head. I now know how a belfry feels after the last chime has rung, and my mouth feels like an unswept barn floor. Luckily, to-day is Sunday. I hope no-one noticed me dozing in church.

Despite the way I feel, I must record my impressions of last night's event while they are still fresh, if a little hazy, in my mind. I feel that Arthur's betrothal comes too soon; Lucy Westenra has been truly dead for less than a year, and the horrors of her final moments haunt my dreams even now. It was Arthur whose strong hand put her to rest; can he really have put the whole affair behind him so quickly?

I think not. I believe this engagement is a spiritual balm. I think he will be grappling with poor Lucy's ghost for years before she lets him be.

All this said, I must admit that I can understand Arthur's attraction to this delightful woman. She is closer in age to Arthur than was Lucy, who had just turned twenty when she died. Miss Keswick is five-and-twenty, with rich, dark and curly tresses, skin as smooth as cream, and dashing hazel eyes. Her laugh is a silver bell.

My belief that she is after his money is completely misplaced. Her father, who introduced the couple, is worth several of Arthur, who is hardly a pauper. No, prestige is what Eustace Keswick is after.

Though dressed impeccably to-day, Mr. Keswick has never lost the air of the hardscrabble iron digger he once was, and no amount of elocution training can eradicate his strange guttural accent. To his credit, he has realized this, and Amanda has had the finest schooling; but for her independence and verve, she could almost be English.

It was also a relief to see Arthur's home properly decorated again. The Godalming estate could have been a funeral parlor for most of the last year. The drapes were drawn no matter what the weather; crucifixes everywhere, as well as portraits of Lucy. Funereal flowers as well, but with a difference—Arthur placed garlic in every room.

With this new love, all that is gone. Sunshine streamed into the grand ballroom, the crucifixes have been placed to provide a sense of devotion, not protection, and the ghastly aroma of garlic has been purged in favour of lilacs.

I'm afraid I indulged a bit too much in the champagne. I realize this morning that, since the Dracula affair, I have been drowning in my work, and dark, depressing work it can be. I have not taken a holiday in more than a year, and each day I contend with the worst of humanity.

I am certain I embarrassed myself with my empty chatter and rusty dancing. The orchestra was fine; Mozart, Liszt, Chopin and recent popular composers were in the repertoire.

Toward the end, Arthur and Amanda took the floor, and a bit of magic occurred. The orchestra seemed about to take a break, but one of the violinists kept playing, and, I believe, improvising. Instinctively, all the dancers but Arthur and Amanda left the floor; the violinist's aria seemed to be for them alone. At first, he played a lively Hungarian polka, then gradually slowed the tune down, changed the tempo until all eyes were on the betrothed couple who moved beautifully in one another's arms, their eyes locked in love until they, and the music, faded to a stop.

There and then, the match was truly made. Never were a couple more in love for all the world to see, and to applaud in gentle envy. Applause rippled across the room, and attention gravitated to the orchestra stand, but all we saw was the violinist walking calmly away, his back to the audience. We called for an encore, but I think he wanted to leave us with a beautiful memory, for he never did come back. I have no idea who he was.

"You have outdone yourself, Arthur," I said, when I was able to steal a moment alone. "How did you meet her?"

"Actually, I've known her for years. My father was Mr. Keswick's agent in England, and he used to bring Amanda along when he came over for business trips in Europe. Until last month, I hadn't seen her since she was in finishing school, and—"

"Love at first sight," I interrupted.

"Exactly!" Arthur exclaimed. "Have you talked to her? She is charm itself."

"I can see that," I said. "If I may ask a question in my professional capacity ..."

"You're thinking what everyone else is thinking," Arthur replied, his eyes narrowing. "That this is too soon after Lucy. No one mourns Lucy more than I, and no one misses her more. But she is gone, John, and I am not. My life is not over. Have we not had our fill of death, and after-death? Amanda is spring sunshine, and I want that sunshine in my garden."

I nodded. "I hope you understand my concerns. I have loved you a long time, Arthur, and have no wish to see you hurt."

"As a doctor, you should wish to see me healed. Amanda, I promise you, is the very salve."

I clapped him on the shoulder. "Long life and happiness, old friend."

He embraced me. "And to you. Fret not, John, I know what I'm doing."

And so I continued to indulge champagne, joking and dancing until long after a decent man should have come home. It must have been two in the morning when I tried to dictate my last entry. I barely remember what I said, and I'm not sure I want anyone to hear it.

July 5, 1891

It is happening again. Were I as superstitious as Van Helsing, I would believe there is a curse on the Godalming family.

Amanda Keswick, Arthur's fiancee, is being attacked by a vampire. I received a frantic call from Arthur this morning.

"You must come quickly, John," he said. "Amanda's been sleepwalking!"

"Arthur—"

"There are marks on her neck, John. You know what that means."

I made haste to the ornate Langham Hotel near Hyde Park, my stomach clenched and my palms white. This could not be. We hunted Count Dracula across the continent to his Transylvanian lair. We fought off his ruthless gipsies. The Count is now burning in the hell from whence he must have come. He is dead. I saw it done. I saw Jonathan Harker slash his throat and poor, brave Quincey Morris obliterate the vampire's heart with the Bowie knife that I now have on my wall, my only memento of that brave American. The Count cannot have come back. It is not possible.

(Pause.)

The Keswicks are staying in an upper-floor suite, replete with everything a vampire might want; plenty of hand- and toe-holds, a balcony, large French windows, and a susceptible young girl.

I found them in Amanda's bedroom: Arthur, Eustace Keswick, his stout wife Petunia, and another doctor. A bit shorter than I, age I should judge about forty. As he extended his hand to me, I felt an extraordinary sense of *deja vu*. I had seen his likeness before. An athletic man, square jaw, moustache, and the dark eyes that mark the English gentleman. I noticed that he keeps his stethoscope in his top hat. Ingenious!

"May I present Dr. John Watson," said Eustace Keswick. "Dr. Watson, this is Dr. John Seward. Lord Godalming seems to think he has expertise."

"Arthur flatters me," I said.

Arthur muttered a dark comment under his breath.

"A pleasure to make your acquaintance, Doctor," said Watson. "I know of your reputation."

"Are you the hotel physician?"

Keswick shook his head. "He is the most famous physician in London, the companion of Sherlock Holmes."

"Ah." And no doubt charging a fat fee to share the

privilege, I thought. I wonder if Keswick knows that Mr. Holmes is dead?

"I have made my examination," Watson said. "I should be eager to hear your impression."

"Wouldn't anyone like to hear my impression?" asked the patient.

Amanda Keswick was sitting up in bed, pouting prettily and probably reconsidering her engagement. "I think this hotel has rats. I had some sleepwalking episodes when I was a little girl, and I think this long trip from home has stirred me up!"

"Seems healthy enough," I said to Arthur.

"Just take a look at her neck, will you?"

I did, and involuntarily gasped. Two sharp, deep puncture wounds, spaced about as far as normal human canines would be, and of the type I have seen on only two other victims—Lucy Westenra and Mina Harker.

"Arthur is right. This is serious," I said.

"I may be in agreement with you," said Watson. "Could we confer in private?"

We stepped into the vast sitting room. Keswick closed the door, and indicated the decanter on the elaborately carved mahogany sideboard with a protruding black eyebrow. Watson immediately poured two brandies and offered me a cigar. I took the brandy, but declined the cigar.

"I have seen such wounds before," he said. "Clearly, so have you. Lord Godalming has discussed his experiences with vampirism with me already, and on one occasion before. I should like to hear what you have to say."

As briefly as I could, I told poor Lucy's story, and then

asked him, "Where have you encountered this phenomenon?"

"In Transylvania, at Castle Dracula."

I felt my jaw drop, and took some brandy to steady my nerves. Watson then told me his own extraordinary tale: the search for Jonathan Harker, the discovery of a dead, bloodless child, the attack the three vampire sisters made upon Sherlock Holmes. He explained Holmes' theory that the women were wearing false teeth filled with belladonna extract. Comforting thought, but he did not see Lucy Westenra vanish into mist and glide through a keyhole at her tomb.

"I think we are the victims of fraud here," Watson said. "That girl has lost no blood."

"But she will, mark my words," I replied. "It took Lucy weeks to succumb, and that was due only to our intervention. How did Miss Keswick come by her wounds?"

"She spent last night dining with Lord Godalming," Watson said. "Afterward, he put her in a hansom with directions to this hotel. A very agitated man hailed the cab and offered double fare to get to the Langham as quickly as possible. Miss Keswick saw no harm in it, and let him in. That is the last thing she remembers before arriving here."

"And the man?"

"Nowhere to be seen."

"What did he look like?"

"Tall, thin, black hair, piercing gaze, cloth cap, dressed in black—the very description of the Farringdon Street Ghoul, as he is called by the newspapers. It is at times like this that we need Sherlock Holmes. Instead, we must settle for Inspector Lestrade."

"I take it, Doctor, that you still believe in the fake teeth?"

"He pierced her neck, yet apparently did not drink her blood, or very little of it," said Watson. "No one, not the doorman, nor the bellman, nor her parents noticed any blood on Miss Keswick. The wounds weren't discovered until her mother found her wandering in the hallway, apparently sleepwalking. Though her eyes were open, Miss Keswick seemed to be in a dreamy state. Mr. Keswick said that her pupils were constricted. Something that argues, incidentally, for some kind of drug."

"She was also somewhat nauseous, according to Arthur, and to me that argues for a vampire attack," I replied. "What did Arthur say?"

"Lord Godalming and I are not the warmest of friends. He frustrated an investigation Sherlock Holmes was keen on finishing, and I was witness to a most unpleasant altercation between the two."

"I'm sorry," I said. "He never told me."

"The question is, what to do now?"

"Keep her bedridden and seal the room with garlic," I said without hesitation. "Otherwise, she will surely die."

To my surprise, Watson nodded.

"I think it will bring peace of mind to your friend," he said, "and it will give the wounds a chance to heal. Shall we come back in, say, two days?"

"That should be sufficient to gauge her progress."

"Very well, then." We shook hands, and gave our joint opinion to the family.

"I will not!" cried Amanda Keswick. "I feel perfectly fine."

"It's only to ensure that the wounds don't fester and

develop an infection," said Watson soothingly. "These wounds are unusual. If you go out and about, we don't know what might get into them."

"I concur," I said. "Stay within the confines of the hotel until Saturday, and then we'll see. Of course, if something does happen, then contact one of us right away. And don't forget to put garlic on the windows and doors."

"Thank you, John," Arthur said, tossing a hard, quizzical glance at Dr. Watson. Turning to his betrothed, he added, "Trust me, this is for the best. I won't put you through poor Lucy's hell if I can stop it."

Amanda bit her lip and turned away from him. I am ashamed to say I felt some relief at this; I still don't think Arthur should be married right now.

So now we must watch, and wait.

* * *

Note, Amanda Keswick to Her Parents

July 6, 1891

Please don't be angry with me when you find this. I am not ill, and Arthur's concerns notwithstanding, I resent being treated like a prisoner in a satin cell. All this vigilance is stifling me, and it is not pleasant to hear Arthur bellowing at Dr. Watson. I need to clear my head.

A few moments ago, as I lay reading in my room, I heard the sweetest strains of music coming through my window. It was a melody that was familiar, and yet which I could not place, until it struck me: it was a softer, slower version of that *impromptu* dance the other night, when Arthur and I seemed to be floating on clouds. The violinist is in this hotel, and his playing calls to me. I want him at the wedding. (Though if I am held prisoner in my bedroom much longer, I grow less certain that I want one.)

I must know who that man is, and I am going out to meet him. I expect to be back before you find this note, not more than an hour at the most.

Your affectionate daughter,
Amanda

CHAPTER FIFTEEN:
A VAMPIRE IS DISPATCHED

Dr. Watson's Journal

July 7, 1891

The darkest secret of all is now in my hands, and I don't know what to do.

I had just finished examining Amanda Keswick, who is in the pink of health. Her neck wounds had almost healed, contrary to the expectations of Dr. Seward, and I told her parents there was no reason to keep her locked up during this fine summer weather.

Godalming disagreed completely, of course, and after a rather loud row ordered me never to visit the girl again, an injunction I have no intention of obeying.

Deciding it would not be best to go home in a foul mood, I stopped at the Langham bar for a stiff whiskey, and was delighted to see old Sergeant Adams, whose wounds I treated at Maiwand. We drank and reminisced for about an hour or so, and made plans to meet again when we could take more time.

As I rose to go, the sight of Amanda Keswick dashing through the lobby caught my eye. She burst onto the street and hailed a hansom. As it pulled away, Godalming came onto the street and hailed the next one. Curious, and just drunk enough to be bold, I did the same.

"Try to get ahead of the cab in front of us and follow

the one it's after," I told the cabbie. "Get rid of the other if you can."

"Cost you."

I handed him a fiver.

"Right you are."

I could have saved my money. The streets grew more familiar as I realized Miss Keswick's destination had so often been my own, and my heart pounded in wonder as her cab pulled to a halt in Baker Street in front of that familiar building and source of wonder and adventure to which I still had my key: 221B.

Up the seventeen well-worn steps she climbed as I lurked across the street in the shadows. The cabs left, a few minutes passed, and then the soft glow of a lamp appeared in the sitting-room window. In it, behind translucent curtains, appeared two silhouettes, that of the girl—and of Sherlock Holmes!

My heart stopped. I did not comprehend how this could be possible: I had examined Holmes' body closely and personally pronounced him dead. I readied his body for transport back to England. There could be no doubt. Some impostor, or perhaps even a twin brother Holmes had never told me about, could be the only explanation, for, as he so often told me, when you have eliminated the impossible, whatever is left, no matter how improbable, must be the truth.

They stood close together, talking, and I saw the girl offer her neck to him. An impostor then; Holmes was never capable of that sort of intimacy. I dashed across the street, hoping to surprise them.

As stealthily as I could, I tip-toed up the steps, skipping the step that creaked and always told Holmes I was on my way. As I climbed, soft violin music sounded in my ears, and the style was unmistakable: Holmes had somehow come back.

Now my pulse pounded and my throat contracted as a thousand questions formed in my mind. I heard Amanda's voice softly in the dark.

I gently opened the door and stepped inside.

The music stopped abruptly, and Holmes gazed at me and then snapped his head away.

"Leave, you fool!" he snarled. "You'll ruin everything!"

"My dear Holmes!" I cried. "You're alive! It isn't possible!"

"You're right, Watson. It isn't possible, and I'm not alive."

With that, he turned his face fully toward me, and my Lord, it was a hideous sight: Holmes, and yet not Holmes. His face was paler than I would have thought possible, even for him, and his vampire canines had come back, sharpened to hideous, glistening points. His eyes blazed red in the dark, recalling our encounter with Count Dracula. Even from the doorway, I could tell his breath was foul.

I felt my heart sink with horror and sorrow, my feelings reflected in Holmes' sad countenance.

"Leave us, my dear," Holmes said. "You have your instructions."

"Yes, sir," the girl said meekly, and retired up the stairs to what had been my bedroom on the next floor.

"For God's sake, Holmes, will you tell me what is going on?"

"Not that you need more whiskey, but pour yourself one anyway and sit with me one last time, old friend.

You've been working too hard of late, my dear Watson; I fear you've been spreading yourself too thin."

"What do you mean?"

"You've been all over London to-day. You visited Lestrade at Scotland Yard, saw your usual patients in Kensington, and you just came from the Langham, where you have been carousing with an acquaintance you encountered unexpectedly."

"Holmes! You astonish me!"

"I thought you needed reassurance as to my identity. How did I do?"

"You are right in every particular."

"The mud and dust on your boots gave me most of it. You usually have one or two whiskies before retiring, but tonight the aroma is powerful, which means you have already had more. Since you are not given to drunkenness, I infer that you saw someone you knew in a bar, and your prompt arrival after Miss Keswick tells me it was the Langham."

"Astounding."

"Elementary. I was hoping not to bring you into this, Watson. I did not want you to bear the shame and the revulsion of what I have become."

"A vampire." Even uttering the word, I still found the idea incredible.

"Yes. And also the Farringdon Street Ghoul, as Fleet Street has chosen to call me."

My throat tightening, I said, "Tell me what happened, Holmes. Didn't you die with Moriarty at the Reichenbach?"

"Yes, that's the last thing I remember from life, my hands throttling that scoundrel Moriarty's neck as we fell.

I think I cracked my head on a boulder. I don't remember hitting the water.

"But next I remember waking up in darkness. May you never go through this, Watson. To be entombed, alone, in the dark, with no hope of rescue ... I thought I had been buried alive. In panic, I coughed and screamed and thrashed about, and broke the coffin's lock in my fury. This happened on the train, you see, and we were not yet back in London. I stepped out of the coffin, disoriented and incoherent. My senses eventually cleared. When I could see where I was, I was aware of something else: a hideous craving that could only be satisfied by the consumption of blood.

"Instinct had taken over. The sensation is not unlike hunger; if you've gone without a meal for a week, you'll have an idea what it's like. A rat scuttled over my feet. I snatched it like a starved beggar, broke its neck, and opened its veins. And that is when I realized what had happened to me and I came to my senses. When the train stopped to take on new passengers, I sent a wire to Mycroft asking him to make arrangements to collect the coffin, in which I hid, on its arrival in London. He is accustomed to secrets and surprises, though I daresay this set him aback."

"So Seward and Godalming were right all along?"

"Not about everything. My body has been reanimated and changed in ways I don't fully understand."

"How do you ... sustain yourself?"

"I have yet to take a human life, if that's what worries you. Even in this condition, that is something I will not do. Self-denial, as well you know, is second nature to me. Did I not starve myself once for three days in order to fool you? I may be a monster, but I am not a murderer. Animal blood does not suffice, however; it is the thinnest broth when a hearty stew is needed. And so I have been forced to the shameful deeds so well chronicled in the papers. I lurk wherever blood is likely to be flowing, and partake of what I can. Fortunately, I can often go as long as five days between feedings, but the craving never goes away."

"There must be a solution."

"Oh, I have one. Miss Keswick is at the center of it."

"You haven't—"

"No, no my dear fellow, but that is what I want Godalming to think. This can't continue."

I forced myself into a professional demeanour.

"I don't know what you have planned, but at the very least I must examine you, Holmes. The more we know, the better able we will be to handle others of your kind."

"Sound thinking, Watson. But first, let's send Miss Keswick home, shall we?"

I called her name up the stair, and the young woman drifted slowly down. Gone was the verve and fire she showed when I visited her this morning. Now, the wounds had been freshly opened and trickles of blood were drying. She barely seemed to recognize me; her mind was distant and unconcerned with her situation.

"Get her a cab, will you, Watson? No, don't touch the blood. Once she is on her way, we may proceed with the examination."

"Holmes, have you lied to me?"

"Not in the least. I have not taken anyone's blood myself, and never will."

"Then how did this happen?"

Holmes reached into his pocket and produced the

false vampire teeth he had shown Jonathan Harker so many months ago.

My stomach recoiled when I realized what my friend had in mind. Once again, he would use his own death to rid the world of great evil, and damn the price to those who love him! What must have happened to make this seem a sensible thing?

"I can't let you do it!" I cried. "There has to be a better way!"

Holmes shook his head slowly.

"If this be the price of immortality, it is far too high," he said. "I have spent hours in libraries studying all the vampire folklore I can find. In no instance is there a story of a vampire shedding this curse and rejoining human society. It is the stake alone that can free him. How long can I continue like this? And I am doomed in any case."

For the only time in our long acquaintance, I heard self-pity in his voice.

"Sooner or later, I must succumb to these cravings. Sooner or later, I will create new vampires whether I desire to or not. Godalming has a hard heart, a steady hand, experience, and he despises me. Once he sees Miss Keswick, he will want me dead. His hatred of me will accomplish what his love did for Lucy Westenra. Once the deed is done, vampires will walk the streets of London no more."

"Holmes, I—"

Holmes crossed the room with surprising speed and spun me toward the door.

"I am sorry to end our partnership like this," he hissed, "but you must not interfere. Let me end my pain."

I looked into his black, bloodshot eyes. The thing that

looked back at me was not Sherlock Holmes. It had his features, his intensity, his voice. But the soul, the passion for justice, and most of all the humanity were now nothing more than a dying coal in the chamber that once held a warm and human, if distant, heart.

He was right, and I knew it. I did not resist, and I had no stomach for the task I had just proposed. Who could I tell? Seward? Van Helsing? Still ...

"Just one thing, Holmes." I extended my hand. He took it, and I placed my other hand on his wrist, where the pulse should be. To my astonishment, he had one: much slower than one would expect, but a pulse nonetheless.

"Holmes, if there is a chance—"

"There isn't, John. Go back to your wife, your practice and the morning sunshine. Promise me that when you write your memoirs, think of me as a creature of this great and grand city, not a lurker in the night. Take the girl and go."

Reluctantly, I led the listless Amanda Keswick back to the street. Her cab was still there; evidently it had been instructed to wait.

"Have you been paid?" I asked.

"Not for the next trip, sir."

"Take the girl back to the Langham. There's a fiver in it for you if you don't tell anyone there that she was here."

"Very good, sir."

July 8, 1891

I slept fitfully, my dreams filled with strange creatures of the night, of my dearest friend looming over a helpless woman with gore dripping from his fangs for much of it.

Toward dawn, though, I became aware of a slow,

rhythmic thumping in the back of my head. The vampires faded, and I was back in the lecture hall at the University of London. Old MacGillivray stood before us, indifferently mapping out the nervous system as was his way.

MacGillivray was a beastly bore, the sort of lecturer who presented the material as dryly and monotonously as possible, rarely revising it unless forced by events and new science to do so. He droned like an industrial loom.

"The autonomic nerves are responsible for the day-to-day functioning of the human body," he said drearily, lightly tracing his pointer across the anatomy chart. "They regulate everything from the irises to the heartbeat—"

I jolted myself to attention.

"—blood vessels, glands, lungs and similar organs function without using our conscious thoughts in order to do so. But the autonomic system is linked to the conscious mind. If we become angry or aroused, that will increase the heartbeat."

MacGillivray buzzed on, the thumping continued, my interest began to wane, and my head nodded as it so often did during his dreary lecturing. But on waking, his description of the autonomic system lingered, as did the measured, steady heartbeat that did so much to lull me off. I wrote down everything I could remember before the dream faded completely, but the thing that lingered was this: the heartbeat is an autonomic nervous function.

The slow, steady pounding was Holmes' pulse as I remembered it.

So what is the nature of vampirism?

All of a sudden, I understood in a flood of hot perception. Magic had nothing to do with vampirism! Vampirism is a disease, one that somehow reactivates the nervous system after death. The body's functions resume to a limited degree, but with one critical difference: it can't manufacture blood. It can't eat as we do, it can't sustain itself. It must obtain its blood from outside sources.

This explains the newly-grown teeth, the slow pulse, the foetid breath.

Now the darkness of superstition has been put aside in place of a plausible scientific theory, and there was no scientific researcher more tireless than Sherlock Holmes. Where there is a theory, there is hope; where there is a disease, there is a cure.

I dressed in haste, and made sure my revolver was loaded.

"Call Dr. Jackson for me, Mary, and see if he can take my patients to-day," I told my wife. "No time for breakfast!"

The sun was bright and the air thick with a grayish, sulfurous haze as the hansom dashed over the cobbles toward Baker Street. The heat was oppressive, and my shirt soaked with perspiration by the time we rounded the corner. My heart banged in my head when I recognized the Godalming crest on the coach parked in front of 221B.

An angry and astonished Mrs. Hudson stared at me in fear and fury as, gun in hand, I pounded up the stairs toward the ominously ajar door.

"I'll explain later!" I cried as I jumped past her.

A figure appeared in the doorway: Seward.

"Dr. Watson, I—"

"Back away, Doctor," I said, pointing the Webley's barrel straight at his nose. "You two are about to make a drastic mistake."

"Arthur!" he barked.

Godalming came out of Holmes' bedroom, no blood-stains on him, thank God. He wore the drab, dusty clothing of a workman. He might have been a gardener.

"What are you doing?" he demanded.

"I am a doctor and an old Army man, Lord Godalming. I know how to use this, where a bullet will hurt the most and exactly what it will do at close range. Please sit down, and keep your hands where I can see them."

Mrs. Hudson hesitantly poked her head in the door.

"Ah, Mrs. Hudson," I said, forcing myself to calm down. "I believe some tea would be welcome about now, wouldn't it, gentlemen?"

"Dr. Watson—"

"All in good time, Mrs. Hudson. All in good time. Tea for three."

"Ver- ver- very good, sir."

"I take it Holmes is in there?" I asked Godalming.

"He's in a coffin on the floor."

"Sit down, gentlemen."

I outlined my theory.

"Come now," Godalming said. "How do you explain the Count's ability to transform himself, or Lucy's turning herself into mist and drifting into her tomb?"

"I don't believe those things happened, my lord," I replied. "You were deceived; how, I cannot say. Seward, you have the facilities we need to study this. We can keep Holmes under observation, we can—"

"You're mad!" Godalming snarled, rising from his chair until I swung my barrel in his direction. "You haven't seen what he's done to Amanda!"

"He's drugged her," I said. "Seward will tell you she's lost no blood. Take a look on the chemistry table. Go on. I won't shoot."

Godalming approached the acid-scarred table with its tubes, flasks, and burners and saw, as I did now that there was sunlight, that it had been in recent use.

Mrs. Hudson came in with the tea tray, setting it down on the sideboard. I put my revolver on the right arm of my chair, where it would be within easy reach, and poured the tea myself. Mrs. Hudson slipped out.

"John, what's this?" he asked, motioning Seward over.

Seward examined the tins on the table.

"I'd say he's been making a heroin solution," Seward said.

"A little more believable than vampire visitations, what?" I said. "He injected it into Miss Keswick with false vampire teeth."

"But why?" Godalming asked, confused. "What purpose could all this serve?"

"He wants to make you angry enough to end his torment, my lord, with your stake and hammer. He does not know he has a disease."

"And you don't have a treatment, Watson."

Our heads swung toward the bedroom door. A ghastly, pale and weak Holmes, clad in his familiar mouse-coloured dressing-gown, hovered in the doorway, his hands clasped behind his back.

Both Godalming and Seward thrust crucifixes at him. Holmes walked blithely by and took his usual armchair by the fireplace.

"I'm afraid I grew up without the benefit of Catholic superstition," he said blandly. "Dracula and his acolytes may have taken to heart the fallacies of medieval times, but we modern vampires are made of sterner stuff. I'm afraid I didn't hear all of your theory, Watson."

I reiterated what I told the others.

"So you see, Holmes, there is a good chance that you have a strange and unique illness. If we can discover its nature, we can discover its cure. We can end vampirism and the barbaric practices surrounding it."

"Have you worked out how to keep me supplied with blood while we work on this?"

"That does present a certain difficulty."

"Nor can we say how long it will take to obtain results, if ever."

"Do you prefer the alternative, Holmes?"

"I do!" Godalming cried, snatching my pistol, levelling it at Holmes' head and firing; he had been edging towards it while I was otherwise occupied. Holmes dodged to the right and the first bullet missed. The second struck something metal in the side pocket and ricocheted, hitting him elsewhere on his body. Holmes' eyes bulged and blood spurted from his mouth. He doubled over and collapsed.

Enraged, I cracked Godalming hard across the jaw, felt a tooth or two loosen, but that brought no satisfaction. I struck him again, this time in the nose, and would have beaten him into a bleeding, unrecognizable side of beef had Seward not pulled me off.

"Stop it! Stop it, man!" Seward cried. "It's over! It's over!"

Godalming fell to the rug, gasping and bleeding. Hot tears streamed down my face as Mrs. Hudson's heavy feet stomped quickly up the stairs.

"Mr. Holmes! Dr. Watson! What could have—"

And then she saw the carnage.

I placed my arm around that good and stalwart lady's shoulders and gazed at my friend's bleeding body. Whether he was alive or dead, I could not tell.

"I'm so sorry you had to see that, Mrs. Hudson," I said as softly as I could.

Godalming rose shakily to his feet.

"I'm sorry, Doctor Watson," he said. "It had to be—"

"It did not!" I snapped. "We had a chance to rid the world of a horrible scourge and save one of the finest minds this century has produced! You just sent us back to the Middle Ages!"

"Let's go, Arthur," Seward said. "I'll fix you up. Please leave Mr. Holmes to me, Doctor. I am in a somewhat calmer frame of mind."

My heart broken, I sank into my chair and stared at the broken, unmoving body of my closest and dearest and most admirable friend, truly gone now. So much adventure. So much heartache.

"Mrs. Hudson," I said at last, "please summon Mycroft Holmes. We can't let a word of what happened get into the papers. There would be riots. And though this may prove next to impossible, I implore you not to say a word to anyone."

"Not to worry, Doctor Watson," she said, covering the body with a blanket from a closet I'd forgotten. "Please join me for a cup of tea downstairs. I'd just like to sit a moment and remember him. I need someone nearby right now."

Unable to bear more, I took a last look at the corpse on the floor, shuddering as spots of blood began to spread across the blanket and the icy hand of sorrow gripped my heart. It saddens me to think that my last memory of Sherlock Holmes will be one of a horrid, violent death. Let the matter rest in Mycroft's hands; the Holmes stoicism will surely see him through.

"I can do no more for him now," I said, patting Mrs. Hudson's hand, "but I can be make sure he will not be forgotten."

CHAPTER SIXTEEN: THE GREAT HIATUS

[Editor's note: For the full facts relating to the murder of the Hon. Ronald Adair, refer to Watson's published account of the case, "The Empty House." I have omitted them here for the sake of brevity. —SS]

Dr. Watson's Journal

April 6, 1894

The fullest flower of the English language cannot express my feelings on what I can only describe as the miracle of yesterday. For the first time since I cremated my beloved Mary, there is sunshine, nay, a bright new star, in my heart. Even now, I cannot fully believe it; and this is just as well, for only the most charitable of readers could accept what has happened. These facts will likely never see the light of day.

But the irrefutable fact remains: Sherlock Holmes has returned from the dead!

I had spent much of my day at No. 427 Park Lane, the scene of the murder of the Hon. Ronald Adair, a minor nobleman who usually spent his days at the city's card tables, generally without spectacular successes or failures. The fact that he had spent the last game of his life at the table with the notorious Col. Sebastian Moran aroused my suspicions, of course, but though I applied the methods of my old friend to the best of my admittedly limited ability, I could not work out just how a murderer could get into

Adair's upstairs den, lock the door, shoot him in the head and escape unseen and unheard, unless Colonel Moran had somehow developed the ability to take invisibly to the air.

On my way home I bumped into a stooped, elderly bookseller and caused him to drop some of the books in his arms. I apologised and thought that was that, but he followed me home, thanking me profusely for helping him pick his books up from the cobblestones. To be truthful, his manner began to annoy me, but he directed my attention to a gap on my bookshelf, which he offered to fill with some of his stock. I moved my head to look at the cabinet behind me.

When I turned again Sherlock Holmes was standing smiling at me across my study table. I rose to my feet, stared at him for some seconds in utter amazement, and then it appears that I must have fainted for the first and the last time in my life.

Certainly a grey mist swirled before my eyes, and when it cleared I found my collar-ends undone and the tingling after-taste of brandy upon my lips. Holmes was bending over my chair, his flask in his hand.

"My dear Watson," said the well-remembered voice, "I owe you a thousand apologies. I had no idea that you would be so affected."

I gripped him by the arm.

"Holmes!" I cried. "Is it really you? Can it indeed be that you are alive? How is it possible? You were twice dead when I left you!"

"Wait a moment," said he. "Are you sure that you are really fit to discuss things? I have given you a serious shock by my unnecessarily dramatic reappearance."

"Dramatic" was hardly the word. The last time I saw

Holmes, he was a dying vampire, lying in a bleeding heap on the floor of 221B as my Webley smoked in the hand of Lord Godalming. I closed my eyes for a moment and opened them. My old friend still stood there, alive and breathing. He had somehow beaten his hideous disease. Again I gripped him by the sleeve and felt the thin, sinewy arm beneath it.

"Well, you're not a vampire, anyhow," said I. "My dear chap, I am overjoyed to see you. Sit down and tell me how you came alive again."

He sat opposite to me and lit a cigarette in his old nonchalant manner, looking even thinner and keener than of old, but there was a dead-white tinge in his aquiline face which told me that his life recently had not been a healthy one.

I bombarded him with a thousand questions, and here I condense his answers:

"Had you stayed upstairs rather than tend to Mrs. Hudson after Lord Godalming shot me, you would have seen me stagger to my feet after about an hour or so. His bullet was deflected off the derringer I had hidden in my gown, but that slowed it down enough so that it lodged in my breastbone. A subcutaneous wound; I removed the bullet myself later. Vampires can be resilient creatures.

"By the time Mrs. Hudson arrived with Mycroft, I had formulated a plan, one which I hope you will understand and which pleases you.

"Mycroft and Mrs. Hudson agreed to keep the Baker Street rooms as they were, pending my return if I was successful, and we all agreed to keep silent until the time was right. The world already presumed me dead, which I was, and there was no need for anyone to believe otherwise.

"Your theory gave me a new mission, for you were right, my dear Watson. You've read Darwin?"

"Of course."

"I believe vampirism serves an evolutionary function; in a way, it serves as life's last chance. While a living person carries the disease, it lies dormant. But it is activated once the body dies. Incubation takes about three days. If the body is still somewhat intact, many of the autonomic functions resume. But the host must supply the blood, which is why the canines develop. Once the disease is purged, they are no longer needed, and the body replaces them, as it does when a child grows into adulthood."

"I'll take your word for it, Holmes."

"Watson, if you had told me more about this phenomenon in the first place, you might have saved me months!"

"You know perfectly well you would have thought me mad," said I. "You had already surmised that some ancient alchemical potion of Dracula's was somehow responsible. That fit better with your existing theory."

"Indeed. Anyway, as you so ably surmised, vampirism is a disease, and a curable one," Holmes continued. "Armed with this insight, I made my way to a laboratory in Montpelier, France and toiled from sundown to sunrise for two years before I made the finding critical to understanding the virus. And here—" he placed a vial on the table "—is the cure."

"What is it?"

"A garlic derivative. I still don't know why garlic is so toxic to vampires, but the virus's reaction to it is extraordinary. Treatment was painful and terrifying at first; after all, I had mostly myself upon which to test my progress.

Hard enough to even find vampires; harder still to find vampires willing to subject themselves to laboratory analysis, but I flatter myself to say that I have restored several to full human health. Rarely have I encountered creatures so grateful. Perhaps, Watson, you should track them down; they have stories to tell, believe me, especially the older ones.

"I almost killed myself several times, but I was determined to prevail. My bliss knew no confines when my canines fell out and normal teeth began to grow. But I knew I had truly succeeded when I passed a bakery on my way to the laboratory and the aromas from the ovens insinuated themselves deep within my nose and awoke in me the fiercest hunger, the first time I had desired food, genuine, human food, since the Reichenbach. There is no way I can make you understand the joy that filled my heart when I salivated for sustenance that wasn't blood! I bought and devoured an entire baguette."

"How did you control your craving for blood?"

"I forced myself to subsist on beef and pork blood. But as I made progress and the disease waned, it became easier."

"That still leaves a year unaccounted for."

"I am never far from my Stradivarius. I needed to accustom myself into normal life again. So if, in your readings, you have come across the name of a Norwegian violinist named Sigerson, then you have a fair account of my doings."

"Speaking of which, how do I explain your return to the reading public?"

"Don't."

"What?"

"Nothing would be gained, and much would be lost. How can I act as the last and highest court of appeal in the realm of detection if you tell everyone I was a vampire? Surely the reading public has had its fill of me in any case."

"You haven't seen my correspondence. Dead or not, they clamor for more adventures every day."

"Not for a while, then. Let me regain my normal life first. And that starts with the Honourable Mr. Adair, and yet another echo from the Reichenbach. We shall soon visit Colonel Sebastian Moran. I imagine he'll be rather surprised to see me. But first a word with Dr. Seward is in order."

* * *

Dr. Seward's Diary

(dictation transcribed from wax cylinders)
April 9, 1894

Today I had the most extraordinary shock.

I had just returned from lunch with Lord and Lady Godalming when my secretary handed me a card.

"Another one who thinks he's Sherlock Holmes, sir," he said. "He sure looks the part, though, have to give him that. He's waiting in your office."

The figure who greeted me—tall, slender, and gaunt, with an aquiline nose and square chin, in the familiar frock coat—was indeed none other than Sherlock Holmes, whose bleeding body I had last seen sprawled on the floor of his Baker Street flat.

"Mr. Holmes?" I asked, my voice rising half an octave. "How is this possible?"

He extended his hand and smiled. In somewhat of a daze, I accepted it, and it was warm. He laughed at the wonderment on my face, and I saw, with awe, that his teeth were smooth, yellow with nicotine, and even.

"Mr. Holmes, I cannot find the words. You are a wizard, sir! They would surely have burned you at the stake four hundred years ago."

"I'm afraid it is dull, pedestrian science that takes the place of wizardry," he said, taking a seat and offering me a cigarette as if I were in his office. I declined the cigarette and boldly took his pulse. It beat in his arm, strong and regular.

"No ghosts need apply," he added.

"There is no doubt," I said. "Every trace of the vampire appears gone from your body. It is as though you were never cursed."

"I was never cursed," he replied, "I was diseased. Watson's theory proved correct, you see. Vampirism is a virus. Once it is introduced into a host, it lurks quietly until the host dies, to awaken once blood no longer flows. After an incubation period of three days or so, the virus reactivates the nervous system."

"I see."

"The body lives, but it cannot sustain itself as before. Blood must be obtained from without."

"But the other things," I said. "The fear of Christ, the transformations into animals, the lack of an image in the mirror—"

"Your idolatrous talisman had no effect upon me, if you'll recall," Holmes replied. "The vampires in Transylvania spent their original lives when religious mania in that part of the world was at its height, and that's what they were reacting to. They had hundreds of years in which to reinforce their beliefs. I do not believe they can transform themselves into animals or mist, for I have been unable to do so. Hypnotism, magician's tricks and superstitious hysteria can account for it. But I will allow the possibility that perhaps the unlamented Count had mastered dark arts we will never understand."

"And the lack of an image in the mirror?"

Holmes hesitated.

"I never lost my image. I must put that down to superstition as well."

I doubted he was telling the truth, but what could I say?

"Why did you come here, Mr. Holmes?"

"To give you this." He placed a flask and a thick envelope on my desk. "The cure for the curse. It is derived from common garlic. I have also prepared you a copy of my notes, the formula, and the treatment I inflicted on myself and some others. I can only hope that a qualified physician can come up with a more humane course of treatment than did I. Naturally, you may consult me freely."

I took the flask in my hand as if it were the Holy Grail.

"The cure. Van Helsing will never believe it."

"I doubt that he will want to. Please give my regards to Lord Godalming and extend my apologies to his wife. My heart is not hardened against him; indeed, he performed exactly as I wished. I hope someday he will do me the honour of sharing his company again."

"You are an extraordinary man, Mr. Holmes."

"You are perceptive, Dr. Seward."

And with that, he donned his top hat and strode from my chambers. Again, I marveled at the gift he had given me, and my eyes filled with hot tears as I thought of Lucy.

ABOUT THE AUTHOR

STEPHEN SEITZ has been writing professionally for most of his adult life. Except for 13 years in the Washington, D.C. area, he has always lived in Vermont. He went to Washington after graduating from the University of Vermont in 1978, where he met his first wife and had a son, independent filmmaker Dan Seitz. While in Washington he worked as an editor and researcher in the U.S. Department of Education; technical writer and editor for a company under contract to the U.S. Department of Justice; and analyzing statistics and writing reports under contract to the U.S. Department of Energy. He became a journalist after returning to Vermont, and his work has appeared in newspapers and magazines all over New England. He also wrote *Getting Started in Small Business Advertising*, which is available now at Simplyaudiobooks.com. He lives in Springfield, Vt. with his wife, Susan. This is his first novel.

Mountainside
Press

*Mountainside Press
publishes
outstanding Popular
Culture books that
examine the ways
people live, learn
and express themselves.*

*Phone (802) 447-7094 • Fax (802)447-2611
www.mountainsidepress.com*